Tread Softly

Kate Pennington

**Hodder
Children's
Books**

A division of Hodder Headline Limited

For Venetia Gosling, friend and colleague,
whose expertise and support I could not have done without.
Very many heartfelt thanks.

Had I the heavens' embroidered cloths,
Enwrought with golden and silver light,
The blue and the dim and the dark cloths
Of night and light and the half-light,
I would spread the cloths under your feet;
But I, being poor, have only my dreams;
I have spread my dreams under your feet;
Tread softly because you tread on my dreams.

W. B. Yeats

One

'Mary, my girl, listen when I tell you!'

Mary Devereux ignored her father's voice and continued to stare out at the white frost laid thickly on the branches of the oak tree. It was December. Winter had taken hold.

'Mary, bring me that parcel of tawny silk from the window ledge.'

John Devereux came and shook her. He took the bolt of silk back to his workbench and began to cut long strips with sharp shears.

'Mary, Mary, dreamer Mary!' her cousin Hal mocked, as he passed by.

She tossed her head defiantly.

Hal grinned and tapped her forehead. 'What goes on inside there?'

'What do you mean? I was looking at the frost on the tree, that's all.' Mary didn't reveal that the intricate pattern of the branches reminded her of the delicate lace used to trim the gowns and cotton shifts which her father made. Nor that the sheen of the ice on the pond had the quality of silver silk. Hal would have laughed and said she had strange thoughts.

'The girl's no use to man nor beast,' Hal muttered, and went to deliver a message to his own father, David.

'Sir Sydney wants to buy in extra fine kersey for his winter hose. You have to ride into Plymouth, to the cloth merchants by the harbour.'

The under-tailor left off work at his loom. 'When would that be?'

'Yesterday!' Hal joked. 'You know Sir Syd!'

His father frowned. 'I'll go directly. And Hal, don't speak lightly of your betters; you don't know where it might land you.'

'In the stocks at the very least.' Mary sneaked in a sly comment.

Hal aimed a light cuff in her direction, which she dodged. 'I'm needed back in the kitchen,' he said with an air of mock self-importance. 'Else I'd stay and teach you better manners, cousin!'

Mary's high laughter followed him between the rows of workbenches where a dozen tailors and seamstresses worked. Many exchanged a few words with Hal, who always gave as good as he got.

'. . . What's for supper tonight, Hal? Will you put by a slice of best venison for me?'

'Yes, if you'll save me a seed pearl from the cuff of that glove you're making!'

'. . . Hal, when are you going to come courting at my window?'

'When the moon eclipses the sun, and not a day before!'

'Ah, Hal, how you break a girl's heart!' came the sigh, then more laughter as the red-haired youth bowed low and made his exit.

'Mistress Mary, give a hand with this collar,' Bess called. She was the one who had pretended to be lovesick for Hal. 'I can't thread this wire without you holding this end for me.'

Then it was, 'Mary, run for an extra length of silk ribbon.' And, 'Go ask the kitchens to boil some wheat for more starch!' Or, 'Whatever will we do without whalebone busks to flatten Lady Anne's stomacher?' Then, 'Mary, search for horn in the outhouse. Horn will have to do instead!'

All day Mary ran and kept warm at her tasks. And all day she dreamed. She lost herself in times gone by, when her mother had sat amongst the women, and had been at the very heart of Mary's existence.

'Child, we must restrain these curls,' her mother had said.

Mary was a maid of seven when her mother sat her in the sunlight by the cottage window. Her black hair hung round her shoulders, glossy and thick.

Her mother had twisted and braided the wild clusters and pinned them neatly under a cap of brown kersey made from a scrap which John had brought in from the workshop. 'There!' she had murmured, half-satisfied, half-sad. 'Now you are a proper little woman!'

Mary recalled the quickness of her mother's nimble fingers as she'd smoothed and divided the tangled curls. There was the smell of starched linen about her, and the scent of bread rising in the warm hearth. She remembered not liking the tight, nipped feeling of her newly braided hair; how she had complained and shaken off the cap, tugging to release the curls.

'Lady Anne will not like to see them,' her mother had scolded. 'She will call you a wild thing and send you to live with beggars at the roadside!'

'Why do only beggars have curls?' Mary had asked her father later that evening. She would not want to beg by the road, she confessed, and have only the rinds of fruit and stale bread to eat.

She remembered her mother's slow smile and the shake of her head as she said, 'Child, child!' and stroked Mary's cheek as she laid her head on the pillow. Her touch was soft as the silks in the workroom, and more precious by far.

'We are the lucky ones,' Bess was saying now to her neighbour. Old enough to be Mary's grandmother, still she teased the men and threatened to make a fourth husband of each and every one. She was as wide as she was tall, solidly encased in horn corsets and swathed about with emerald green skirts. 'Sir Sydney keeps us fed and clothed, though we work by candlelight and ruin our eyes at this close work.'

'Praise be,' Marion said, without enthusiasm.

Bess clicked her tongue. 'And what if we *are* kept uncommonly busy because of this invitation to court? It is an honour for the family, and if our work is good it will reflect well on us.'

'But how will it serve us?' The disgruntled Marion had that day suffered the sharp end of her mistress's tongue. 'Will it put extra food in our bellies and feather down in our pillows? No, before spring I will find myself a husband who will keep me. I'll not be beholden to her ladyship one day longer than needs be!'

'Hold still, Mary!' Bess scolded, as the young girl's hand shook from holding a thread of seed pearls in place against Lady Anne's new collar. 'Yes, and you'll live on thin porridge the rest of your life, Marion,' she told her.

'I'll find me a rich husband with a hundred head of sheep to his name!' Marion protested. 'Then young Mistress Mary here can come and keep house for *me*, while I travel to market on a fine horse to buy shoes of Spanish leather!'

'Yes, and I'd steal your rich husband with his hundred head of sheep,' Mary claimed. 'For I shouldn't want to keep house for the rest of *my* life neither!'

'Vixen!' Marion scolded with a loud laugh. 'This is what comes of a motherless child!'

Motherless. The harsh word jolted Mary back into the past. To a day when the oak tree had been heavy with acorns, and the boughs had almost touched the ground.

Her father had returned to the cottage as the sun was setting. There was no smell of a cooking pot over the hearth, the fire was unlit.

'Mary, where is your mother?'

'Gone to gather reeds for baskets,' Mary had replied. She had stayed at home to pick apples from the tree.

Together she and her father had gone to search for her mother. Sir Sydney's steward had come riding across their path. 'Don't take the child near the lake!' he'd warned.

But John had ignored him and hurried on. Mary remembered the reed bank and people splashing into the muddy water; ducks flying clear with a loud beating of their wings; her father dropping her hand and rushing ahead. She had stood and watched as the birds flew low across the ruffled water.

'John, she's stone cold!' the men had said as her father pulled the body of his wife into his arms.

Mary's mother hung limp and pale. She'd lost her cap, and her hair hung loose. Now they would send *her* to be with the beggars for showing her wild curls, thought Mary numbly.

'She's long drowned,' someone said.

'Aye, poor mistress.' A woman at the water's edge had wrung her hands and cried. Mary's father's heart had broken before they prised his wife away from him. They'd buried her in the Campernowne graveyard and Sir Sydney had ordered a Latin engraving for her headstone.

'A widower is only half a man,' Bess had said.

But the others had laughed and said that, try as she might, she would never make John Devereux her husband number four.

Now Mary knew that it wasn't the curls that had brought about her mother's death, though for years it had been her fixed belief. God had taken her, not the beggars. It had been an accident; no one ever knew exactly how she'd drowned. Only that the steward, Hugh Trevor, had discovered her body floating face up in the lake, her long dark hair spread out like a fan, her arms wide and making the shape of a crucifix, buoyed up by her thin summer skirts.

'Lady Anne!' came the announcement at the door of the workshop.

Heads went down, the gossiping stopped. As head tailor, John Devereux went and greeted the great lady of the house and her two daughters.

They came with their heads held high, their long necks white as a swan's, with pinched mouths and suspicious eyes. Their gowns swept the threads and cuttings along the wooden floor.

Mary retreated to her window seat, hoping not to be noticed.

'Kathryn and Jayne wish to see their court gowns,' Lady Anne announced in a voice as narrow as her waist.

'Your Ladyship, we have the patterns but not yet the gowns,' John explained. 'We have two pairs of satin bodies in white and silver already made: one for Kathryn and one for Jayne. I myself have sewn in the pearl adornments with thread of gold.'

The young ladies sighed and complained at the lack of progress in the workshop.

'These we have seen,' Lady Anne reminded the master tailor. 'What of the colours for the gowns? And should they be loose or closed? What is the latest fashion at the court?'

'For that you must ask my Lordship's steward,' John replied. 'Hugh Trevor is recently returned from Oxford and has spoken with the wife of George Carew, who was at court but lately.'

'Hugh Trevor never notices such things as ladies' fashions!' Kathryn protested. 'All he cares for is horseflesh!'

From her quiet corner, Mary observed the oldest daughter. Below average height and of slight build, her fair hair was concealed behind a high satin headdress edged with gold trim. Her forehead was broad and clear, her complexion white as could be, so that her large grey eyes seemed the most prominent feature of her perfectly oval face.

'Hush!' her mother warned. 'But what is the Queen's favourite colour of the moment?' she persisted. 'What shade of red, be it carnation or flame, peach or maiden's blush?'

'I will not wear red!' Kathryn asserted. 'Red signifies deception!'

Then it would suit! Mary said to herself. She had grown up with the older girl's spite and lies.

'Only if it be yellow-red, my child.' Lady Anne took up the paper pattern on John's table. 'I like this shape for a closed gown for Kathryn, if closed gowns be the fashion.'

'With pinked edges and paned sleeves!' the girl cut in. 'And puffed Chinese silk through the slashed bodies.'

And a gag of finest taffeta for the mouth! Mary thought, with annoyance. It pained her to see such demands being pressed on her father. And with so little respect!

'My gown must be as fine as Kathryn's!' Jayne insisted. 'I will not be overshadowed because I am the younger!'

'You should wear turquoise from head to foot,' Kathryn shot back. 'Turquoise signifies jealousy, and you are the most envious of sisters!'

'White and silver will suit.' Lady Anne overrode the squabble with a flick of her long, slim fingers.

'With ermine,' Jayne insisted, who, although only fourteen years old, knew as well as anyone the cost of such trimming. 'Greenwich is by the river. It will be a cold fog, and I shall need my garments to be lined with fur.'

John bowed his head and remained silent. Since autumn her ladyship had been fretting over the apparel for the family's brief court visit, obtained through an old friendship with a rich family in Oxford who themselves hung on the outer skirts of court life. Sir Sydney himself had at first refused the invitation on the grounds of expense, but his wife and daughters had set up such a howling that he had soon capitulated. 'I shall not attend myself,' he had insisted. 'But if my wife and children see fit to ruin us with bills from haberdashers and goldsmiths, who am I to deny them?'

He'd ridden out to the hunt and returned with a roe deer. 'This is what comes of having a woman on the throne of England!' he'd confided to his steward as he threw down his cloak. 'Now every lady dresses like a queen, from merchant's wife to baroness.'

Lady Anne was deaf to her husband's sarcasm. Between October and December of the year 1581, partlets of jewelled lace and French hoods with billaments of pearls occupied her every waking thought. 'My daughters will be presented at Greenwich,' she said. 'Every eye will be upon them.'

Accustomed to these impatient, quarrelsome visits to the workshop, Mary no longer feigned interest. Instead, she would sit quietly with some white work on her lap, knowing that by seeming busy she would escape notice. Here, where the light was good, she could draw threads to pucker the surface of the fine linen, then begin to embroider flower motifs linked with flowing scrolls, all executed in dainty split stitch. Then, if her father took Lady Anne and her daughters off to a far corner of the long workroom, she could let her mind drift. She could look outside at the sloping lawns of the estate all covered with hoar frost, and see the frozen reeds standing like sentinels at the lakeside.

Today the sky was clear blue – there was no breeze. And yes; the fine twigs of the distant trees interlaced like the work on a fine collar. They sparkled like diamonds in the sunlight, though nature far outshone the work of the human hand. No man, nor woman, would ever capture its delight, Mary thought, though many times she wished that she could.

Two

'Wake up, Mistress Dreamer!' Hal knocked loudly at the diamond-shaped pane and shouted through the window.

Mary gasped and shook herself. 'I wasn't sleeping!' she mouthed back.

Hal grinned and gestured for her to come outside.

'Shan't. I'm busy.' Busy with pulling threads and puckering and stitching. Busy with her dreams.

Outside the window, Hal mimicked a child in a bad humour stamping her feet.

Mary pouted and turned her back, but her cousin tapped again.

'Look who's come a-courting our Mary!' Bess cried, her broad red face wrinkled up into a smile. She wielded her small scissors like Cupid's dart, aimed it at her own ample bosom then feigned a fainting attack. 'Oh my, the arrow of true love unmans even the stoutest heart!'

Mary tossed her head in disgust. 'Bess, *you* may court anything in doublet and hose, and do as you please, but I don't count my cousin Hal as a proper suitor!'

'Quite right, Mary,' her father said with a smile. Then to Bess he added firmly, 'She's a child yet, and I'd thank you to keep that nonsense out of her head a while.'

'She's thirteen, at my count, and ready for a fine romance,' Bess muttered, though John's rebuke had subdued her.

'Come out!' Hal insisted, rapping the pane again.

Sighing and casting a haughty eye on Bess and the other seamstresses, Mary made her way between the work benches. 'What is it?' she demanded of Hal, who by this time stood at the door.

'My master cook needs fish for supper,' he told her, matter of fact, with a straight face.

'Then go and fetch it yourself.'

'I have herbs to chop and pastry to roll.'

'And so it's *my* task to go riding into town through the frost?' she demanded. She was annoyed by the mundane errand which would put an end to her warm, quiet remembering. 'Why me? Why not the potboy?'

'Cod and herring,' Hal told her stubbornly. 'I knew that your services were not in high demand here in the workshop today, and so I informed Master Jeremy.'

Mary frowned. 'May you chop your fingers along with the parsley! And – and may you boil your head to make the pie!'

Hal laughed as he led her down the side of the great house into the yard at the back. 'Put on your cloak for the journey. The horse is saddled and ready. Oh, and be sure the fish is caught today, for there's nothing worse than stale herring to eat!'

Allowing Hal to lift her into the saddle, Mary could find no more insults to fling at him.

Instead, she set the pony towards Plymouth and prepared to make the cold ride. 'In any case, it keeps me out of the way of my Lady Anne and her daughters!' she muttered, knowing that the ladies planned to return to the workshop that afternoon to continue stitching their fine lawn shifts. Their presence would stifle the pleasant chattering that usually filled the room. Kathryn would yawn and complain endlessly, Jayne would bicker and whine, while Lady Anne herself would find fault and work herself into a distress over the length of Bess's chain stitch or the colour of her couched work.

So Mary settled into the journey, noting the noisy starlings quarrelling in the bare trees by the roadside, and the chill of the sea wind blowing directly into her face. The horse, Hazel, trotted smartly, despite the banging of the empty baskets hanging as panniers behind the saddle. Keeping to the grass verges and avoiding the slippery stones embedded in the muddy lane, she soon brought Mary within sight of the church towers of Plymouth.

And it was not much longer before they entered the narrow streets, where carriers with wagons deposited goods at the inns, whence they would be collected by merchants' men who would transport the bales of wool and parcels of fine cloths, the precious metals and herbs, the leather and jewels to the great capital city of London.

Mary conjured with the names. London: Southwark Inn was south of the river; a spot where more carriers met the goods and took them across the bridge which spanned the wide River Thames. Thence along Fish Street to the Mitre Inn, and at the end of their journey, these goods would be hauled off the carts and taken into the goldsmiths' shops of Cheapside and the cloth markets of Blackwell Hall. Names that carried such resonance; names that Mary had heard of through her father and her Uncle David, places that she would probably never visit.

'The Queen has built a trading palace second to none,' John had told her. 'Men gather to sell their goods between marble pillars, and shops stand one on top of the other; milliners above jewellers, hairdressers above shoemakers, and the whole house is named the Royal Exchange after our mighty Queen.'

Mary would sigh and try to picture the scene. But she had no desire to purchase any of the riches of which she heard tell. Rather, she would dream of the making of the jewels and the fashioning of the silken suits, for the craft was to her more interesting than the wearing.

'Is London noisy?' she would ask.

'A din of carts and cries, of sailors calling from the river, and of chapmen selling pots and trinkets.'

'And does it smell worse than our town?'

'*Much* worse. For the sea air does carry away the foul stench of the ditches, but in London the air is stagnant and the crush of people ten times as bad.'

Secretly, Mary thought that the smells of London could not be worse than Plymouth harbour's stink of fish.

'And why then do people crowd to the city?' she would ask her father.

'To make money, child. For that is the beginning and the end of it.'

'What do you lack, mistress?' Apprentices called to Mary now as she rode her horse towards the harbour. They held up goods to entice her into their shops: plates of dull pewter and bright silver, worsted stockings and perfumed gloves.

Mary peered into the dark interiors, glimpsing shelves of goods dimly lit by candlelight.

'Come inside. We have cambric linen and dowlas. You can buy it by the ell!' An eager lad sprang to bar her way. His teeth were crooked in a face marked with pox; his dark hair sprouted at all angles from his head.

'I have no need of your common dowlas!' she replied, turning Hazel down a side street. 'I am here to buy fish!'

The disappointed apprentice catcalled after her. 'May your fish rot before you carry it home!'

Mary went on through the dark, narrow ways, where the roofs of the houses almost touched overhead. The unpaved streets were muddy and the gilded signs of the tradesmen creaked on their iron hinges.

'We have your polecat and cat, your black and grey rabbit, your squirrel and your fox!' came the cry from inside a skinner's shop.

Mary glimpsed the back of a small lady dressed in a fashionable tub skirt, so wide at the hips that she must have entered sideways into the shop. The woman said something inaudible in reply to the skinner's offer.

'For banquet wear we have your mink, your sable and your miniver, though it will cost you sixty-six pounds and twelve shillings to line your cloak in such as these!'

The man almost rubbed his hands at the thought of such extravagance. 'But of course my Lady Carlotta, fresh in from Spain only last week, never blinked an eyelid at the price of your lynx, and I know for a fact that her husband's estate is not half the acreage of yours, my Lady!'

Crack! Mary imagined the sound of a trap being snapped shut as the woman fingered the most expensive pelt on the counter.

Then the salt smell of the sea grew stronger and the alleyway opened up to a wide cobbled area piled high with baskets, coils of rope and heavy anchor chains. Gulls screeched and wheeled over fishy remains, while boys ran here and there with bare legs and feet even in this mid-winter cold.

Mary dismounted and tethered old Hazel to a rusting anchor. She knew that at low tide, as now, she must descend the steps running down the side of the sea wall on to the pebble beach, where the fishermen would be found gutting and cleaning their morning catch. Sure enough, she found half a dozen men still at work, and small piles of silver fish with round, staring eyes heaped on flat stones awaiting the knife.

'Master Jeremy, the cook at Saltleigh Hall, wants cod and herring for this night's supper,' she told the nearest fisherman, making sure that all the others could hear.

The man nodded non-committally. 'You must tell Master Jeremy that it's the early bird that catches the worm.'

'Do you mean to say that I am too late?' she inquired. Out of the corner of her eye she saw three men in a rowing boat head for the shore.

'This catch, and that of all the men working here, is bound for the "Anne Archer" and the "Falcon", anchored offshore,' he replied.

'Then it seems that all at Saltleigh must go hungry.' Interested by the tanned look and easy manner of the men in the boat, Mary waited for the other fishermen to gather round like hungry gulls.

'I take it you don't believe what I tell you.' The fisherman wiped down his hands on his leather apron then folded his arms.

'This is a great deal of fish for the sailors to eat,' she pointed out, expecting to have to bargain hard for her supper.

'There are upwards of seventy hands on each vessel, awaiting Her Majesty's command.'

'Yes, and no one to command them,' another of the local fishermen said. 'For Raleigh is forbidden to sail again, and Gilbert rests idle at home in Limehouse.'

'Bid the Queen make *me* captain,' the first man joked as the oarsmen set foot on land. 'Let her send me to heathen and barbarous lands and return a hero. *I* would not then quarrel and find myself flung in the Fleet Prison, as some I can name!'

The newcomers overheard the slur, as had been intended. 'Then you would face without flinching waves as tall as your main mast, would you?' one challenged. 'You would set foot on foreign land like Raleigh and Gilbert, and return in glory with precious metals and jewels?'

'Try me!' the fisherman boasted. 'For then I would be *Sir* Peter Greenfield, and all the misters of Plymouth may go hang!'

'Raleigh is not yet Sir Walter,' the second sailor reminded him. 'He is just now returned from Ireland, where he was slaughtering Spanish mercenaries.'

'Aye, and wenching from Dublin to Connemara, by all accounts!'

Mary heard the argument darken with all this talk of killing and wenching. She began to feel impatient to secure her supper. Taking one of the fishermen aside, she bartered for enough fish to fill the bellies on the Saltleigh estate by promising further trade. 'If Master Jeremy hears well of you, you can rest easy that he will come back for flounder and plaice long after the "Anne Archer" and the "Falcon" have set sail for the Americas.'

The young man thought a little and agreed to sell her his catch. 'Tell the cook to send a maid as pretty as you the next time, and he shall have all the fish he pleases!'

Mary blushed, then bridled. 'I'm not for any fisherman to lay hold of in his net!' she retorted, high-stepping up the stone stairs and flinging down her panniers to be filled.

The men laughed between themselves.

Meanwhile the brown-skinned sailors took as much fish as they required and prepared to row back to their galleons.

Two of the fishermen, including Peter Greenfield, were left with their slabs still piled high with cod; a fact which pleased Mary as she loaded Hazel with her purchases.

Then she set off through the darkening day, glad to leave the harbour side and wind her way through the town, back along the country lanes to Saltleigh Hall.

'A visitor is expected at the big house!' Marion's news interrupted Mary as she warmed her stockinged feet at the workshop hearth.

Outside, the sky was dark and clear, though snow was promised during the night.

'Mistress let it slip when she worked with us this afternoon,' the excited seamstress went on.

'Marion, leave me be. Can't you see I'm tired and hungry?'

For a while, Marion went on collecting scraps from the floor, but then the expected event got the better of her. 'Aren't you curious to know who it is?' she demanded.

'Very well, who is it?' Mary sighed. Though what it had to do with her and the likes of her she couldn't make out.

Marion put on a tone of extreme mystery. 'We don't know, see! All we heard was that a visitor is coming tomorrow and that it's a gentleman!'

'Hmm.' Mary wiggled her toes then slipped them back into her shoes.

'As I say, that was all we heard; not the name exactly, because Lady Anne spoke it in a whisper, and we could tell that she wasn't best pleased.'

Mary yawned, as if bored.

'Oh, you're a lost cause, you are!' Marion complained. 'Why don't you jump up and ask a hundred questions like any other girl would?'

'Very well, how could you tell Lady Anne wasn't about to welcome her visitor with open arms?'

'Because she had on a sour face when she dropped his

name, and Mistresses Kathryn and Jayne shrieked in dismay, and said "How could Father do this, with us so near to being presented at court!" and suchlike.'

A smile lit up Mary's face. But 'Hmm' was all she said.

'Hmm! Hmm!' Marion mocked. The young woman liked to tease Mary. 'Bess thinks it must be one of Sir Sydney's hunting companions for the ladies to dislike him so. But I say no; for a mere coarse huntsman would not tread on the girls' toes nor make her ladyship look as if she's been sucking lemons.'

'Marion!' John remonstrated, overhearing the seamstress's gossiping as he locked up the scissors in an oak chest for the night.

Behind his back Marion made such a puckered face that even Mary burst out laughing. 'I'll wager this visitor is more troublesome than a mere ale-quaffing huntsman,' she whispered. 'And I shan't sleep a wink tonight for wondering who it can be!'

'Then I shall sleep them for you,' Mary said. Warmed by the embers and weary after her journey, she could have fallen asleep right there by the fireside.

'He'll be a gentleman!' Marion repeated. 'And to my mind, a young and handsome one, with a Spanish cloak and a padded doublet, pinked and slashed and braided. His trunk hose will be coloured with new dyes from Persia, and his ruff all starched and underpropped up around his long, swan-like neck . . .'

Mary's eyelids drooped and her head nodded forward.

'His suit will all be of cloth of tinsel,' Marion predicted. 'He will wear eighteen gold buttons down his chest, each costing seven shillings, and his hat will be of the very best beaver . . .'

'Come, child,' John said, taking Mary by the hand. 'I see that you at least can survive this mystery until tomorrow morning!'

Gratefully she followed her father out of the workshop, waited for him to lock the door then, arm in arm under the starlight they sought their cottage and the warm beds awaiting them.

Let the others dream of their gentleman visitor. Mary's own sleep would be fresh and pure as the clear night air.

Three

Next day, as usual, Mary flitted from workshop to great house to kitchens on her father's errands. The sky hung heavy with grey cloud, the ice thawed and dripped from the high roofs, forming puddles in the courtyard, while a cold, wet mist crept into old Bess's bones and made her curse the winter days.

'Her Ladyship lacks silver points for the sleeves of her tawny gown.' John had taken the message from an anxious maid. 'Mary, you must choose six from the chest and deliver them to her dressing-room!'

Mary did as she was bid, entering the house by a back door and slipping up a spiral stairway to deliver the tiny metal tags.

The Italian maid snatched them and hurried into the bedchamber. 'Follow me!' she muttered to Mary. 'My Lady's humour is not to be borne alone!'

Reluctantly Mary entered the bedchamber, where the four-poster bed lay in disarray, its coverlet falling on to the floor, a mass of lacy garments strewn across its width.

'Give me the points!' Lady Anne demanded, examining them closely and deciding that though they differed from the ones she was used to, they must do the job for today.

'Sophia, lace me tight,' she ordered, 'and after that fetch me the petticoat skirt of embroidered crimson velvet.'

The harassed maid rushed to accomplish her task.

'For God's sake, girl, don't squeeze the breath from my body!' her Ladyship snapped.

Mary looked away to hide her frown. If Lady Anne desired tight lacing, she must pay the price of discomfort.

On went the silk stockings and garters, then the red leather shoes.

'Prepare a paste of almonds,' Sophia told Mary in an undertone, 'while I dress the hair.'

Once more, Mary accomplished the task, which was to moisten the white powder in a small silver dish.

'Such a pulling and tearing!' Lady Anne complained as her hair was combed.

Sophia bit her tongue and shaped the fair hair over a wire frame, which she secured with laces. Then a French hood bordered with rubies was set on top.

'I must be made ready within this half hour!' her Ladyship sighed. 'And though I do not relish this visit from our cousin, still I *will* look my best!'

Mary took in the word 'cousin', and determined to pass on this scrap of information to Marion.

'Scour her Ladyship's face with the paste,' Sophia ordered Mary. 'You have seen me do it often enough. Lay it on even and dab it dry with a napkin.'

Nervously, Mary stepped forward to rub in the white mixture. It covered the pink flesh with a thin white layer which gave Lady Anne's face a blank, mask-like appearance.

'Don't miss a single spot!' came the petulant command, along with a glance from the suddenly opened eyes. 'Who are you, girl?' she inquired crossly.

'Mary Devereux, your Ladyship. My father, John, is tailor to Sir Sydney.'

'Ah, the motherless girl!' Lady Anne dimly recalled the tragedy in the lake. 'You grow quickly, child.'

Mary lowered her eyes and stepped back.

Then Sophia swept in with a heavy gold necklace and agate bracelets, followed by an open gown of white satin embroidered with thread of gold.

'Now the rebato, and don't fumble!' Lady Anne ordered.

The maid assembled the stiff collar with pins, and then, with more pins, attached lace cuffs to the wide sleeves.

'Girdle!' her Ladyship snapped, raising her arms with difficulty as a gold chain hanging with bejewelled scissors, knives, bodkins and seals was attached to her waist.

Then the final order: 'Fan and gloves!'

At last the great lady was made ready to meet her guest.

'And all for Walter!' she declared in disgust, looking to the heavens and hurrying from the room.

A weary Sophia had swept the lace garments from the bed and loaded them into Mary's arms, sending her to the laundering room with an undeserved scolding. 'How slow you are, and how clumsy. And why do you let your curls escape from your cap? Such vanity will do you no good.'

Then I'll chop off my hair! Mary thought angrily. Rather than be judged vain, like shallow Kathryn and Jayne, she would seize the scissors and hack off the unruly locks.

'You must hide your pretty looks,' Sophia said more softly as Mary headed out of the room. 'I have been in the service of many a lady, both here and in Florence, and none are pleased by a shining chestnut eye and sweetly curving lips in those who attend them.'

With a glance over her shoulder, Mary marked the Italian woman's severe black and grey dress. She nodded to show that she understood, then slipped away, running lightly down the stairs . . . and bumping into none other than Hugh Trevor, head of all the serving people at Saltleigh and manager of Sir Sydney's estate.

'We are to gather in the bread kitchen!' the potboy cried, as the steward brushed Mary to one side and the lad ran at his heels. 'There is news of the visitor!' he gasped, round-eyed as a rabbit, scampering along on skinny legs. 'We must gather and hear what is to be done to entertain our guest!'

Mary was swept along the underground corridor in the flow of cooks, gardeners and maidservants, following Hugh Trevor. Still clutching her Ladyship's linen, she squeezed into the warm, vaulted kitchen which housed the giant bread ovens.

'Gather round!' the steward cried above the chatter and clatter of the crowd. Standing on a sturdy bench, with his head held high and hands on hips, he carried his authority effortlessly, as if he himself were superior born.

Instinctively, Mary held back. She found a shadowy corner by the great pile of logs which fed the ovens and observed the tall figure clad in black.

'Within the hour a guest will arrive here at the Hall!' Trevor announced. 'He is a man of importance, and must be served according to his status.'

People nodded eagerly, for a visitor brought variety and was the focus of much gossip. Besides, the cooks would mix herbs and spices into the meats from special recipes, and, with luck, the leftover scraps would evade Sir Sydney's hounds and find their way into the servants' hall and thence into the bellies of the kitchen wench and the potboy.

'He is a great adventurer, a true son of Devon,' the steward continued, with an air that conveyed that he himself was an honoured companion of the expected guest. 'And though fortune has turned its back on him a while, still he has friends in high places.'

Mary frowned at Trevor's neatly trimmed beard and gold earring. Why she had no liking for the man she could not tell, except that she remembered the cold expression on his face when he'd warned her father not to take her by the lake. He'd looked down from his horse, knowing that her mother was drowned, and his eyes had been like stone.

'Who is the visitor? Give him a name,' people muttered.

But Hugh Trevor worked them like puppets. 'Devon has not a more bold explorer! With seventy men he sailed to the New World, to the Cape Verde Islands, on a voyage that few men could undertake. Besides, he is a scholar and poet, a master of prose and sonnet.'

'He speaks of Sir Humphrey Gilbert!' someone guessed.

'No, it is Grenville, fresh back from the Irish wars!' another said.

It is none of those, Mary thought. For the name was Walter, and he was cousin to the Campernownes.

'The Earl of Oxford is his companion,' Trevor boasted. 'And my Lords Leicester and Walsingham presently speak for him at Her Majesty's court!'

There was a gasp as great names dropped from the steward's lips.

Hugh Trevor smiled and at last delivered his audience from their suspense. With a wide gesture of both arms which swept his cloak back from his shoulders he made his final announcement. His mother is Katherine

Campernowne, sister to our own Sir Sydney. His father resides at the great house in Hayes Barton. And so I need hardly tell you that our visitor expected at Saltleigh within this half hour is none other than the renowned Walter Raleigh!'

'Is that all?' Bess blew out her cheeks and made a horse's snicker with her lips. 'Puh, I've dandled little Walter on my knee, before he ever thought of going to sea and making his fortune!'

In spite of herself, Mary had flown across to the workshop with news of the visitor. 'His name is Walter Raleigh!' she'd announced, with something of the steward's pomposity. 'He's companion to the Earl of Oxford!'

But the older women had poured scorn on the information. 'We thought of an earl or a duke,' Marion tutted, 'or at the very least a man of nobility.'

Then they all fell silent as Kathryn and Jayne suddenly appeared at the door.

'We know of whom you were gossiping!' Kathryn's disdainful voice carried down the middle aisle. 'So there's no need to stop just because we're here.'

John and his fellow tailors snipped and slashed at cloth in the uncomfortable silence that followed. Bess sewed furiously, her needle flying through the delicate silk.

'If you did but know, we agree with you!' Jayne said loudly. 'Kathryn and I will do our best to keep out of Walter's way, in spite of our mother's fussing over him. That is why we are here; so as to avoid him at all costs.'

'Hush, Jayne!' the older girl hissed.

'I will not!' Jayne flounced to her padded chair by the window and took up her work with a defiant energy. 'I don't give a fig if Walter sees me sitting here and knows that I have no wish to greet him. Indeed, if he were to speak to me, I should tell him that his presence here casts a shadow over our appearance at court, and that I wish he were at his father's place in Hayes Barton or any other house but ours!'

'Puh!' Bess's lips popped and she failed to conceal a splutter. Marion giggled behind her hand.

'What my sister *means* to say is that the Queen is not pleased with our cousin,' Kathryn tried to explain in a manner less hasty than Jayne's.

'No indeed,' Bess whispered, 'for Her Majesty saw fit to throw him into Marshalsea prison for fighting on a tennis court!'

'Was that not the Fleet?' the irrepressible Marion asked.

Bess spoke from the corner of her mouth. 'That was last year, before he went to Ireland but *after* he sailed back from the New World!'

'Kathryn, the women are whispering!' Jayne declared. 'They must not whisper behind our backs, must they?'

At this Bess straightened her face. 'I'm very sorry for it. And I'm sorry indeed that your cousin Walter has fallen from grace. For a more handsome, winning figure of a man you could not hope to meet!'

'Indeed,' Kathryn said frostily, unsure whether or not the seamstress was playing the fool.

'However, there is one good thing about his visit to Saltleigh,' clever Bess went on. 'Knowing the young man of old; in favour or out, I wager he'll bring news of the latest court fashions with him!'

Slowly the young ladies grasped her point. 'Will he know how long a pair of bodies should be, and how many satin bows to dress it with?' Jayne asked.

'To be sure,' Bess confirmed.

'And whether the French or the Spanish hood is in favour with the Queen?' Kathryn added.

'Most definitely.'

'Men do not notice such things,' Kathryn challenged.

'Men like your father assuredly do not,' Bess agreed. 'But men such as Walter make fashion their Bible, believe me!'

'Thou shalt not wear trunk hose to the knee!' wicked Marion giggled, making fun of the ever-diminishing garment. 'But thou shalt wear them as small pads around the hips!'

Sitting close to Kathryn and Jayne at her usual place by the window, Mary marvelled at the impudence. She noticed her father come to Marion and chide her.

Jayne turned to her older sister to talk in private. 'Perhaps we should pick Walter's brains after all?'

'Since we cannot stop him coming here,' Kathryn said thoughtfully. 'And it's not certain that the Queen will get to hear of his visit, or that she would hold it against us if she did.'

'It's not *our* fault that our cousin is a foolish flatterer with a hot temper!' Jayne pointed out that no blame could possibly be attached to two innocent girls about to be introduced to court life.

There was a short silence, during which the older girl caught sight of Mary sitting quietly nearby. She gave an impatient shake of her head, stood up and went to poke Mary. 'You're a cunning little spy!' she menaced. 'Always there in the shadows, always listening in on conversations!'

Mary flashed her an angry look but said nothing.

'Yes, you're one who would hide behind the arras to learn our closest secrets!' Jayne jumped in, giving Mary a pinch on the arm. 'I'll pinch you till you're black and blue, mistress, if it will stop you spying!'

Flinching, Mary felt hot tears spring to her eyes. But she could not defend herself.

'Listen!' Bess sprang up from her stool, turning it over in her haste. 'Is that a horse and rider I hear clattering into the courtyard?'

Immediately Jayne and Kathryn rushed to the window.

'I don't see anything!' Jayne cried.

'I'm certain it was the beat of a horse's hooves!' Bess approached the two girls and hustled them towards the door. 'You must greet your visitor,' she insisted, 'for now we know that he can be of excellent use!'

'Come, sister!' Kathryn cried, all of a bustle. 'Walter is here!'

As they fell for the trick, John came quickly to his daughter's side. 'Say nothing!' he warned. '*Do* nothing!'

Miserably she nodded and fought back the tears. Then anger got the better of her. She threw down the lace she'd been working. 'They don't deserve such finery!' she retorted sharply. 'They are vain and spiteful girls!'

Her father stared severely at her. 'Control your temper and put on a pleasant demeanour!' he ordered.

'I cannot!' He was asking too much. She felt she *must* give vent to her feelings.

'I say be pleasant, child! For if you scowl and protest, the world will be your enemy, and it will hurt you!'

'I will remember,' she promised, gulping back a deep sob.

'Take a breath,' Marion advised, linking arms and leading Mary to the tall window. 'And look; here's a distraction, for our visitor is truly arrived at last!'

Her remark brought everyone crowding round.

'He's here!' they cried, craning for a better view of the rider who swept up the long straight avenue between the two rows of oak trees.

'He wears a cap of beaver!' someone said. 'His beard is pointed, Spanish style.'

'He has grown into a fair-looking man!' Marion exclaimed gleefully.

As the visitor rode close by, they could clearly see his flowing cloak and under it a doublet of black leather. He sat his horse like a knight of old; upright in his bearing, with his sword swinging at his side, looking neither to left or right but knowing nevertheless that he was observed. 'Look at me!' he seemed to say. 'Am I not a fine figure?'

'Indeed!' Bess sighed, leaning on the door post and gazing out, absent-mindedly patting down her hair as the rider passed by.

'To work!' John said. 'Come away, do!'

With his brother David's help, he shooed the workers back to their tables.

But Mary held her position at the window. She stared through the diamond panes at the dashing rider, catching the click of hooves as the horse entered the courtyard, seeing grooms run to help the visitor dismount.

Walter Raleigh swung down from the saddle, then looked around.

His foot has trodden on the soil of the New World, Mary told herself. His eye has seen great rivers and strange beasts! He has brought back riches untold! Perhaps he has seen a unicorn, or a lion with a flowing golden mane. This is a man who stands astride the world like a Colossus, with such wonders to tell!

Walter glanced up at the myriad windows of Saltleigh

Hall. Then he looked over his shoulder at the grounds he had ridden through, and at the slight figure of a girl standing at the workshop window watching him.

Feeling his gaze, Mary quickly withdrew.

Four

'The Americas!' Hal sighed.

A brave new world.

'I would sail the mighty ocean!' he proclaimed as he scoured pots alongside Jack the potboy. His sleeves were rolled back, his hands red from the freezing cold water. 'I would board Spanish galleons and seize their gold, I would tie myself to the mainmast as storms lashed the deck!'

He and Mary were each dreaming their dreams. She had told him about her glimpse of the great man; how he had swept down the avenue of oaks like a conquering hero. Now Hal was full of excitement and curiosity.

'How does he seem?' he had asked.

'Proud.'

'Tall or short?'

'Tall, with a broad chest.'

'Fair or dark?'

'Dark. His beard is trimmed in the latest fashion. His eyebrows arch like twin ravens in flight.' She laughed as Hal stroked his as yet beardless chin and she saw the greasy water drip from his fingers.

Hal continued to scrub, cursing the accident of his birth. 'Say my father was Sir David Devereux, and my mother Lady Eleanor of such-and-such an estate . . . then I too would seize the chance to make my reputation on the sea. It would not be so hard,' he mused. 'For I'm sure I can command a crew of seventy and slaughter the Catholics in Ireland as well as the next man!'

Mary laughed again. 'But your father is plain David and my father is John the master tailor. I think we must stick to the land and stay safe at home!'

'But, if only!' Hal could still picture himself riding up to Saltleigh Hall in grand style. 'Perhaps being low born is of no account,' he said brightly. 'I shall play the hero in any event, I shall ride my black mare through the oaks and everyone will bow down and say, "Here comes Sir Harold, who was once a kitchen boy, but is now a fine courtier who has set foot in the New World and founded a settlement named after our great Queen. It shall be called New Plymouth, and Her Majesty has bestowed honour and wealth on our own young Hal!" '

By now Mary was bubbling with merriment. 'Why, cousin, this cold weather has affected your brain and you speak nothing but nonsense!'

Splashing out with the dirty water, he pretended to scowl. 'Jack here will be my lieutenant, won't you, Jack?'

'Aye, I will,' the boy vowed. 'Though I may fall sick if the waves rise above my head.'

'Be sick all you please,' Hal muttered, 'but I will not increase your ration of dry biscuit, nor let you lie on the captain's soft mattress.'

'Then I shall not come.'

Still laughing, Mary left the boys to argue and went back to her work. It was less than an hour since Raleigh's arrival, so she was surprised to see Kathryn back in the workshop, her head bowed over her stitching.

'I do not see why all the talk should be of Walter,' Kathryn was complaining to anyone who would listen. 'It's Walter-this and Walter-that with my father. "Walter must have the best meat for supper", "Prepare the best bed-chamber for our cousin, Walter", and so on.'

John Devereux inclined his head politely but made no remark.

'My cousin's head is already too big for his hat,' Kathryn grumbled. 'Why, he has not seen fit to visit us here at Saltleigh for fully ten years, and yet he acts like the master!'

'And did you ply him for secrets about the latest court fashions?' Bess prompted, weary of the monotonous complaints.

'I did, and so did Jayne. We asked whether or not the collar of a gown should be folded back to create revers, and if the partlet should be of gauze embroidered with strawberries, as we have heard tell of Katherine Vaux's court gown. But Walter scoffed and said that this was the fashion of five seasons past, and that if we went to

Greenwich in such garments, we would be laughed out of court!'

Mary sat quietly at her stool and pictured the conversation with some amusement.

Bess tutted and clucked. 'But he offered no news of what was presently in?'

'Only to inform us that ladies of fashion must wear false hair, curled, frizzled and crisped, underpropped with forks and wires and such like!' a disgusted Kathryn replied. 'When Jayne asked why this should be so, Walter went so far as to say that the Queen herself affected this style, and wore a red wig set with feathers and pearls, When poor, simple Jayne again asked why, Walter laughed and said it was because Her Majesty had lost all her own hair from the smallpox, and that beneath the bright auburn wig she was bald as a coot!'

Bess and the other women workers gasped in horror at the scandalous gossip.

'At that I walked out of the withdrawing chamber!' Kathryn declared indignantly. 'I cannot believe such calumny, and I for one will not be wearing false hair at court!'

Smiling to herself at the visitor's bold humour, Mary continued to embroider a silver slip on to a piece of white silk which would form a panel in one of the sleeves for Jayne's court gown. Then, seeing a bustle outside the main door of the Hall, she alerted the others to the party from the house crossing the courtyard towards the workshop.

Soon Sir Sydney appeared, accompanied by Raleigh and followed by Lady Anne and Jayne.

All eyes were on Raleigh; on his haughty bearing, and on every detail of his cream padded doublet, and the dark cloak slung casually across his shoulder which was lined with black sable. The experts in the workshop noted the workmanship and approved.

'What does *he* want here?' Kathryn muttered crossly, gesturing for her sister to come across and confide in her.

'He admired the cut of mother's gown and desired to see the place where it was made,' the younger sister informed her.

Fashion must indeed be his Bible, Mary thought, for him to take an interest in stitching so soon after his arrival.

Raleigh strode down the central aisle, glancing to left and right. He commended David's fine kersey and the hue of its indigo dye. Marion too received a compliment for her arabesque design on to tawny taffeta.

Marion blushed and for once did not look up. Bess bridled as the great man passed her by without comment.

'And here is my tailor, John Devereux,' Sir Sydney said proudly. 'A member of the guild of master craftsmen, and worth his weight in gold.'

Raleigh acknowledged him with the slightest nod of his head. 'A noble calling,' he remarked. 'For where would my lords and ladies be without fine stitching?'

Dressed plain like the rest of us, was Mary's silent response, though she did not find herself disliking the visitor as much as she had been led to expect. After all, his voice was soft and winning, his face fine featured, with a broad forehead signifying openness and courage.

'Ah, cousin Walter, you have learned a great deal about lords and ladies since we last met,' Lady Anne said stiffly.

'Among other things, it has been my privilege to attend court,' he answered with a smile.

'Yes, yes, but tell us about your exploits on the battlefield,' Sir Sydney implored. 'I hear from my sister, Katherine, that you helped rout the Huguenots at Montentour?'

'I was but a boy at that time,' Raleigh said with evident false modesty. 'Fifteen years old and not a day more. But on my return, Father hurried me off to Oxford, into the care of George Carew, lest I kill myself in battle and leave my poor mother grieving.'

'Katherine has had much to bear!' Lady Anne put in with a sigh and a look to the heavens.

'From Oriel College to Law in the Middle Temple,' Raleigh went on smoothly. 'Where I own I learned more of poetry and philosophy than I did of legal matters.'

'Aye, and of women, I'll wager!' Sir Sydney teased.

There was general laughter among the men.

'Sir, we are with ladies!' Raleigh protested. 'Let us only say that the Earl of Leicester was kind enough to notice me. He put me in the way of Queen Elizabeth herself!'

This time the women in the workshop voiced their approval, until the visitor modestly raised his hand and went on. 'I'm afraid I made little enough impression.'

'Pray cousin, tell us why.' Finding her voice, Kathryn pushed home the point.

'Perhaps my tailor in Islington was less skilled than yours at Saltleigh!' Raleigh laughed off the problem.

'Or perhaps the Queen learned of your reputation for extravagance,' Lady Anne suggested quietly. Her white face showed no emotion as she exposed her nephew's weakness. 'It is a known fact that you almost ruined your poor father with your tailors' and merchants' bills, and that my sister in law can scarce find the means to fit herself out in the latest fashions.'

Raleigh found himself under direct pressure. 'Aunt,' he pleaded, smiling, 'you must forgive these errors as a young man's foolishness.'

'Ah, but what of the brawling and fighting in taverns?' Sir Sydney teased again. His question lightened the tone, as did the deep wink of his eye. 'Another young man's pursuit, eh?'

Raleigh had the grace to blush. 'At least Marshalsea gave me the leisure to pen a sonnet or two, hey, uncle?'

'Love poems!' Laughing, Sir Sydney paraded his visitor around the workroom once more. ' "To my most admired lady", followed by her initials. They say you wield a romantic pen, Walter!'

'It seems so, by its successful results!'

'A ladies' man!' Sir Sydney's voice grew quieter as he led Raleigh towards the door.

'With feet of clay!' Lady Anne observed sourly.

'Uncle!' Raleigh said, suddenly turning and facing the large workshop windows. He looked out across a leaden sky where the clouds were buffeted by a strong wind which whistled through the bare trees. 'I have come to Saltleigh to seek a favour.'

'Go ahead and ask it!'

'It is well known abroad that I am not at present the feather in fortune's cap,' Raleigh began.

'Not . . . ? Ah, I see – you are out of favour at the court; yes, yes!' Blustering and chuckling, Sir Sydney let him proceed.

'I lack an invitation to the court,' Raleigh explained candidly. 'If I could but come in the way of the Queen once more . . . you see where I am leading?'

'All too plainly!' Lady Anne snapped. 'And Sydney, the answer must be no!'

A rare frown creased her husband's brow. 'No, sir, I do not see.'

'Well, then, plainly, I wish to accompany you and your family to Greenwich.'

'As I foresaw!' Lady Anne spat out.

Kathryn and Jayne gave sharp gasps and clutched each other by the hand.

'To Greenwich?' Sir Sydney repeated.

'Aye, sir; to attend the court and see the Queen!' Raleigh made his request, ignoring the ladies' consternation and concentrating only on his uncle's bemused face. 'After all, I am part of the Campernowne family; my great-aunt was one-time tutor to the young Princess Elizabeth!'

'You young rascal!' Sir Sydney grinned. 'You want an entry through the back door, as it were!'

'Say no, husband!' Lady Anne insisted. 'It will harm our daughters' standing if it were to come out. The Queen would cast her disapproval in our direction. What hope then of a good marriage for the girls?'

'Nonsense, wife,' Sir Sydney answered, suddenly out of temper. 'It is I who make the decisions, for as the Bible tells us, woman's authority is nil and she must in all things be subject to the rule of men.'

Lady Anne's white mask almost cracked in fury, but she was forced into silence.

Then Sir Sydney turned to his nephew with extreme generosity in his expression. 'You shall take my place at court, nephew.'

'No!' Kathryn gasped while Jayne sobbed.

'What do I want with an invitation to Greenwich?' their father continued. 'I had rather stay and herd sheep with my shepherd or hunt with my hounds.' Turning his back on his wailing wife and daughters, he shook his nephew by the hand and said, 'Yes, yes, Walter, you shall take my place at court and win over the Queen!'

'Why so silent?' Hal asked Mary amidst the cluck and twitter of conversation in the workshop.

It was late in the afternoon. All the candles were lit, casting a flickering light over the benches. Hal had called in to give an account of the banquet being prepared for that night's supper. A pig roasted whole, and with a glazed apple stuck between its jaws. A leg of venison, stuffed pheasant and smaller game birds, flanks of beef and mountains of cured ham. Every fine family in the neighbourhood had been invited to meet Raleigh the great explorer.

'I have nothing of interest to say,' Mary replied. She sewed on in the mellow flame.

Hal considered the moving shadows on her face. 'A Mistress Mary answer to be sure!' he laughed. 'It's my belief that women rarely wait until they have something of interest to say before they open their mouths.'

Mary glanced up. 'And you're a man of great experience, I do believe, Hal.'

He jostled her elbow by way of answer, so she tutted and complained that she must undo her work because of it.

'So do you like our grand visitor, or not?' Hal persisted. 'Surely you must have an opinion like Bess and Marion.'

'I see nothing more than usual to dislike,' she replied.

'Again, typical!' Taking a bobbin of gold thread, Hal twisted it like a wooden top.

His father chided him from across the room. 'At six shillings a reel, that is no play thing!'

So Hal put it down and fiddled with the soft wax around the rim of the nearest candle instead. 'Do you see anything to approve of in Walter?' he asked Mary. 'The shape of his calf, for instance, which is natural and owes nothing to false padding – or the cut of his cloak, the hang of his trunk hose?'

'Take care, Hal!' Marion squawked. 'For I shall faint if you mention such things!'

'I like his wit,' Mary decided.

'Oh, Lord!' Marion laughed. 'You cannot *see* a man's wit. What about his shining eye and barbered beard?'

Mary shrugged and held her ground. 'A man who can recognise foolish vanity in others and use it to his advantage is a man worthy of a certain respect,' she insisted.

It was a remark which caused a flutter of discomfort.

'Foolish vanity!' Bess muttered. 'I hope the child is not describing anyone present in this workplace!'

From his place at the head of the table, John Devereux sighed. 'It is well to remember that walls have ears,' he reminded them, 'and that careless gossip can cost dear.'

Just in time, he quenched the chatter, for who should enter the workshop at that moment but the steward, Hugh Trevor, and the subject of the conversation, Walter himself.

John stood up and bowed stiffly, his joints aching after a long day sitting cross-legged at his work.

Trevor responded briefly. 'Sir Sydney bade me show our visitor more of your work,' he explained, his face as expressionless as Lady Anne's under her mask of white paste. 'What have you in hand, Master John?'

'We are working at gowns for the court,' Mary's father replied. 'Her Ladyship has come to a decision on an open gown of red velvet, with stomacher and matching sleeves worked in gold over ruched gauze, hanging with spangles and seed pearls.'

'A fine choice,' Walter murmured, inspecting the transparent material which John held up. 'And now, Trevor, you may leave me to my own devices.'

The steward's brow creased into the slightest of frowns. 'I am at your disposal until supper, sir.'

'I have no need of your services, however.' The visitor brushed aside the obstacle of Trevor's presence. 'I am at home here in my uncle's house. He bade me treat it as my own.'

Reluctantly the steward retreated, stepping backwards and bowing deeply.

'And now we can be ourselves,' Walter sighed. 'The man walks as if his joints are made of wood, without suppleness. He parrots only what he has been taught.'

Bess let out one of her lip-popping snickers.

Walter turned to her with a smile. 'It is Bess, is it not?' he cried. 'Why, mistress, you have not changed one jot!'

'Bess it is!' Her broad face alive with excitement, the seamstress let go of all ceremony. She came across to the visitor and squeezed him by the hand. 'If laying two husbands in the grave since last we met does not change a woman, then what have I left to fear!'

'Two husbands dead, and still a smile to warm the coldest day! And you, John Devereux, I see you hold your own against the tailors of Italy and France?'

John bowed gravely, refusing the intimacy that the guest invited. 'Sir Sydney is a kind master, sir, and provides good employment.'

'And what of wives, John? Do you run through them as fast as Bess does husbands?'

'My wife died, sir. I do not look for another.'

Picking up a scrap of heavy damask, Walter stroked the raised surface with his long fingers. 'I remember a daughter,' he said in a more serious tone. 'A pretty dark child with rosebud lips.'

'Mary, sir. She is here at her work.' John drew Mary to her feet and formally presented her.

Mary curtsied low.

Walter observed her closely but made no remark. 'I will tell you frankly why I am here,' he said, turning back to John. 'I wish to talk to you about a piece of work.'

The master tailor met his gaze. 'As you are Sir Sydney's guest, I am at your service, sir.'

'I lack a cloak,' Raleigh went on. 'Since I am to appear

at court with Lady Anne and her daughters, it must be a fine one; the finest you can make.'

In the background, Marion raised her eyebrows at Bess, as if to say, 'This guest makes himself very much at home!'

John's eyes gave nothing away. 'A cloak of which style, sir?'

'Spanish, for it is the fashion of the moment. I will wear it across one shoulder, and it must be lined in sable and nothing less.'

'In what colour and material, sir?'

'In jet black velvet, all embroidered in silver and gold. Black is for constancy, and I would signify to the Queen that my love for her is undiminished. And it must be the finest work, studded with pearls and diamonds, fastened with gold clasps to show my undying respect.'

Even Mary could not help but stare. Such a garment was more luxurious than any John had made before.

'The stitching will display motifs from the New World: of roses, iris and pansies, of scorpions, sea monsters, crabs and whales, and in the hem you will work a motto, "*amor et virtute*", which is to say, "love and virtue".'

This time the tailor blinked. 'Her Ladyship visits Greenwich in the New Year, not four weeks from now.'

'And so the cloak must be lined in sable,' Raleigh said evenly. 'For it will be cold on the river.'

'Sir, we must already work by candlelight to make her Ladyship ready. Such a cloak in addition will strain our abilities.' John ventured to point out the major difficulty, despite knowing what the response would be.

Raleigh drew back and stiffened. No more the fond, nostalgic guest revisiting his childhood, but now the complete courtier. 'I charge you with an important task, master tailor. A task which will make your name at the court and enrich your reputation. But your reluctance places a question over your skill. Is it because you cannot execute such a sumptuous garment that you hesitate?'

'It is not, sir.'

'Is it that your workshop lacks the means?'

'No, sir.'

'Then it must be because you think that my uncle is too poor to pay for the pearls and diamonds.'

'I am certain that Sir Sydney gives his blessing,' John replied, though secretly he wondered whether or not his employer realised the full extent of his guest's extravagance.

'Indeed he does. And so your objections are overthrown,' Raleigh said curtly. 'You will make patterns this very evening. I will return after supper to survey your progress.'

With this he turned on his Spanish heels and stalked from the workshop.

'Pearls and diamonds!' Marion breathed as the door slammed shut.

'Pansies and sea monsters!' Bess gasped.

'All in four weeks!' David took a deep breath and shook his head.

Mary recalled the motto: *amor et virtute*. By love and virtue. Walter Raleigh aspired to win back the Queen's favour and on the backs of Sir Sydney's hard pressed tailors and seamstresses. She pitied her father, for no doubt the visitor would prove an exacting taskmaster.

'I will help you,' she told him quietly as David went around the room snuffing candles and creating wisps of acrid-smelling smoke. 'This very evening we will return after supper and prepare the patterns. Do not fret, Father, for you can be certain that Walter Raleigh will have the most beautiful cloak in the entire world!'

Five

'The cloak shall be panelled, and each panel shall have a motif from the natural world,' John decided, as he and Mary sat devising the pattern for Walter Raleigh's cloak.

He laid sheets of thin paper against the black velvet, pinning them neatly then cutting swiftly around the edges. Soon Mary was absorbed in the process of tailoring and then pricking the patterns into the paper.

'Father, since it will still be winter when they go to court, may we work silver snowflakes into the hem of one panel,' she suggested quietly; 'with a robin redbreast atop a bare branch, and the leaves of a holly twig heavy with berries, all combined with golden arabesques and silver spangled scroll work, for the spangles will look like ice, and will glitter in the light?'

John smiled and agreed. 'You should trace the shapes on to the paper so that I can prick them, since the notion is yours.'

Mary's eyes lit up. 'Might I really do that?'

'Child, you have been making pretty designs from nature

since you were scarce able to walk!' John reminded her. 'Why, I would come home to you and your dear mother in the cottage on an evening and find you scribbling with chalk on to slate, and the pictures all would be of flowers and the lambs in the field. The truth is, I would trust you with this design above all others in the workshop!'

Her father's praise may have been the natural fondness of a father for his only daughter, but Mary accepted it gladly and felt it warm her even in the chill, empty workshop.

'I believe Nature's ways entwined themselves early in your heart,' he went on. 'Your eye is keen and your hand steady, your touch is light and delicate.'

'It's a wonder to see the shape of an oak leaf or the dusky pink petals of the rose,' she explained. 'And to work this on to paper, thence on to the richness of silk or velvet; this is above all what I dream of doing!'

They worked on in silence for a while in the light of a single candle. John's head, tinged with grey, was bowed forward, his own fingers working nimbly, while Mary's cap almost touched his shoulder and she gave her whole attention to marking the outline of a tiny bird on to the semi-transparent paper.

'Tell me, child, do you ever long for the touch of silk at your own wrist, or the quiet rustle of taffeta at your heel?' Glancing up from his work, John gave his daughter a keen glance.

She hesitated before answering. 'Such things are not for me,' she said.

'No, but do you not long for adornment, as most girls do?'

Again she thought hard. 'Not so much, for my pleasure is in the making.' For Mary, the wearing of fine gowns, jewels and feathers went along with the shallow vanity which she saw in Jayne and Kathryn. She herself would scorn to show the world such pettiness.

'In your heart,' John insisted, seeming to want to tease her, 'do you not fancy yourself a great lady?'

She grinned across at him. 'And be like Hal, Father? Dreaming of adventures he can never go on? No, I am content to be as I am.'

John smiled back. 'Then I am not fearful for you that you will not hold your own course through life. It is your mother's strength I see in you.'

Then the talking wound down once more as the two basked in their memories, until the peace was ended by the sudden opening of the door, and the figure of Raleigh entered, swinging a lantern and bringing with him the scent of ale and roast meats from the heaving supper table.

'And so I find you faithful to your promise, master tailor!' he cried heartily as he closed out the cold night air.

John greeted him courteously.

'I have brought best ale from the house,' Raleigh declared, bringing a pitcher and two pewter tankards from under his cloak. 'I intend to enjoy your company, John, above that of the invited supper guests, for they are stout and short of wit, being country people for the most part, whose talk is all of sheep and fish – and besides, their breaths smell of the subjects of which they speak!'

'I can talk of cypress silk and cambray cotton, silver points and peascod doublets,' John replied evenly, 'but I fear that will not please a man of your broad horizons.'

' 'Tis better than herrings,' Walter reasoned. 'I wonder how these young farming fellows will find themselves a wife, for they wax poetical about the price of a fleece at market, but all their conversation with the ladies is leaden and muttered into the froth of their ale cups!'

Teasing and laughing, his face flushed from the fire of the great house and by the ale he had already drunk, Raleigh threw himself at Mary's feet. 'Mistress Mary, baa-baa! Pray let me come a-courting, baa! Else I shall bleat into my small beer and shear my hair short as a ram's back for sorrow!'

In spite of her embarrassment, Mary let slip a smile.

'See, the lady admires my wit!' Raleigh cried, jumping up.

'I do no such thing,' she contested. 'I merely enjoy my work!'

'And very fine work it is.' The visitor bent forward to

examine the delicate pattern making. ' 'Tis those small, slender fingers; so pliant and dextrous!'

This time Mary blushed in earnest and fell quiet, while her father frowned at Raleigh's flattery of his daughter and drew his attention back to the noisy departure of the Campernownes' guests in the courtyard.

'They will have a cold ride home,' he remarked. 'The clouds have lifted and the frost has taken hold. But at least there is the moonlight to guide them on their way.'

Mary glanced out at the half dozen gentlemen and ladies who were preparing to leave. Grooms held their horses while they mounted; the horses standing patiently in the frosty night, except one chestnut mare who pulled at the rein and started away without her rider being fully established in the saddle. There was a shout and a clatter of hooves, then the runaway reared up and whirled around, scattering the ladies and making the men curse.

With quick reactions, John seized the visitor's lantern and ran to bar the mare's way out of the yard, leaving Mary alone in the workshop with Raleigh. A gust of cold air made the candle flicker and then extinguish. She gave a gasp, dropped her work and sat quite still in the pitch darkness.

'I see Mistress Mary does not like the dark!' Raleigh exclaimed. 'And neither do I, for it prevents me from surveying her charming, fair-favoured features!'

As Mary found no answer, he continued to tease, dropping courtiers' phrases into the silence.

'My mistress's eyes shine like the stars in the velvet sky!' he declared, seeming to hover ever nearer to her seated figure. 'Her ruby lips are soft as rose petals!'

Mary clasped her hands and almost stopped breathing. This was no longer a joke to her, whatever Raleigh thought. 'Do not jest,' she pleaded, shrinking away.

At once he relented. 'Ah, forgive me, child. The fumes from the ale swim in my head, else I would not have frightened you for the world!'

'Sir, I was not afraid!' she replied, gathering herself together. 'See, the mare has alarmed the rest of the horses.'

The noisy clamour from the yard had increased, and by now, a lady rider was unseated, lying on the ground and crying out that her ankle was hurt. So Raleigh followed John to the rescue, striding out of the workshop and across the yard, then gently assisting her to her feet. The lady leaned heavily on him as he escorted her back into the house.

After a while, Mary began to breathe easily again. Though she had had the wit to find a final retort for Raleigh's foolishness towards her, she had in truth been highly uneasy. True, he jested, but he had been very close to encircling her waist with his arm, and from that, who knew what else might have followed? Would she have pulled away and reminded him of her age and station?

Would it have altered his course of action? Or, indeed, was his amusement merely in causing her blushes? It was too hard to fathom; she did not know enough of the world.

So thinking, she stayed quietly in the darkened room, until the door slid open and two shadowy figures slipped inside.

'We are safe here.' A voice which she recognised as Hugh Trevor's spoke in a half-whisper. 'We may speak freely,' he assured his companion.

'Then let this go no further than your own ears,' the other man hissed back. 'You must understand that I am under instruction from our friends in Rome to make ready our supporters in England and to seize any opportunity to make mischief for the throne!'

Again Mary suppressed a gasp. What now?

'I know this!' Trevor whispered. 'And it is why I brought you here, for Raleigh has found a means to return to court. He is to meet the Queen at Greenwich in the New Year!'

The second man gave a short laugh. 'He intends to find certain favour and win a reward which no man has yet achieved!'

'Aye, there is a secret country to be won, decked out with unplucked flowers and fair, rolling hills!'

Trevor's mocking, sly response confused their listener. Her skin prickled and she shrank further into the shadows.

'But this is good news,' the stranger went on. 'We have worked on Leicester without success, for his allegiance to the Protestant Church holds good against all assault and Rome's words fall on deaf ears. But Raleigh's ears may be more open to our cause.'

'The Earl of Oxford is his constant companion in London,' Trevor reminded the stranger, who was a small, stout man in a heavy, hooded cloak. 'And we know full well that Oxford's true sympathies lie with Rome.'

'Watch closely. If Raleigh succeeds in his courtship of the Queen and gains her trust, then is our time to drop the small, secret seeds of rebellion into his restless, ambitious mind. We will water them and watch them grow, until the healthy vine wraps itself around him and produces the sweet grapes of the Latin mass on his lips and a bitter hatred of that stern Protestant mistress burns in his heart!'

The urgency of the man's voice startled Mary, though his words meant little to her.

'Hush!' Trevor warned, pulling him further into the shadow of the deep, arched doorway. 'If Raleigh can but succeed in ousting Leicester as the Queen's favourite!' he sighed.

Once more, the stranger laughed. 'Elizabeth may be our appointed queen, but she is a mere woman, susceptible to flattery as all that sex. Has Raleigh perfected the art of poetry?'

'He is a master of both prose and poetry,' Trevor laughed back. 'There is no metaphor or simile beyond his reach. But more important, he is driven by overweaning ambition, and will not be downcast by setbacks. He will mount the highest hill and penetrate the deepest jungle if it will lead to rich worldly rewards!'

The same coarse laughter as before made Mary shiver. Only when Hugh Trevor drew the stranger out of the workshop and the two figures melted into the night did she close her eyes, take a deep breath and rise to her feet.

Soon her father returned to take her home.

'Come, Mary; the ice has frozen solid. It is too cold to continue our work,' he told her. 'Raleigh says I must take you home to a warm fire, else you will freeze to death like a robin on the bough!'

'Then who will stitch his cloak?' she asked, in as cheerful a manner as she could muster.

'You're shivering, girl!' John offered her his own cloak and led her out under the stars. 'Are you ill?'

'No, Father.'

'Then what troubles you?'

'Nothing.'

They walked a little way, the ice on the grass crunching under their feet.

'Father, who is Rome?' Mary asked, still trying to piece together the puzzle of Trevor's secret conversation.

'Rome is not a person, but a place in Italy, child.'

'And what does the place signify?'

'It is the home of the Pope, ruler of all who hold to the old Catholic faith. Why do you ask?'

'I only wish to learn a little more, so that I am not so ignorant.'

'Then beware such knowledge,' John told her, holding open the door of their small cottage by the lake. 'Talk of Rome is dangerous in these Protestant times, for it is not beyond the memories of those yet living that the Queen's father, King Henry, broke from the Pope and led England its separate way. He made many enemies among the old families of this land, and there are still some who would overthrow this Queen and lead us back to Rome if the chance arose!'

Mary sighed as she went inside. Though their house was simply made of wood and wattle, with an earthen floor and a rough stone hearth, still she preferred its cosy familiarity above all grand places she had seen. Her father's answers had satisfied some of her curiosity, though why the steward of the Campernowne estate should be conversing with a stranger over such matters still did not make sense.

'Child, you heard what I said?' John persisted. 'It is best not to ask too many questions on the troubled matter of religion. Leave that to scholars and politicians. It is enough that we go to church on a Sunday and offer our loyalty to God and the Queen.'

Mary nodded. There were evidently dark secrets abroad in the world. Kissing her father's cheek, she took to her narrow bed by the single window, rolled herself inside her coarse woollen blanket, then lay down and stared out at the stars, thinking.

Six

The days approaching Christmas were filled with unending toil. From early in the morning, before dawn had broken, until long after the sun went down, the seamstresses in Sir Sydney's tailoring shop worked with bowed heads and nimble fingers, transforming the plain surfaces of silks and satins into intricately patterned panels for pairs of bodies and wide sleeves. Outside, the low clouds and cold mists of early December gave way to clear skies and intense cold.

Mary did not like the short days; the way night drew in before her walk home and the cooped-up, restricted quality of life during a hard winter. But if life was dull for her and her fellow workers, how much worse must it be for the birds in the bare branches? Each morning they came to the cottage window, begging for the scraps she threw down; thin sparrows and bold robins fighting over crumbs of stale bread. Mary would sigh as she watched, shake out her skirt to release the final crumbs, then wrap her woollen shawl around her and trudge towards the hall.

As for the Campernowne family, these were fractious days of bickering and worrying. Kathryn and Jayne were constantly in the workshop, vying for attention from John and his tailors; Kathryn using her position as the elder of the two to bully Bess into finishing the work on her gown before her sister's.

'*Why* must I wait?' Jayne would cry, coming to pester Mary who was sewing the panels of Raleigh's cloak. 'Put that away and take up *my* gown, else I'll tell my mother!'

Mary would try to explain that her father had given orders that she must work continually at the black velvet. 'There is much still to do; I cannot break off.'

Then the girl would fly into a temper, snatching the cloth from Mary's hands, throwing it down and stamping on it, and Mary would be forced to endure the flare-up until it died naturally and Jayne dissolved into tears, at which point Kathryn would sigh and say that her sister was made of bile and choler in equal measure, and that she would never find a husband, no matter how finely she dressed at court.

'Your face is red and swollen,' she would point out with as much spite as she could muster. 'You turn yourself into an ill-favoured child whom nobody will like!'

'And you are vain and proud beyond everyone!' On this occasion, Jayne came back on the attack. 'I heard Father tell cousin Walter that you cannot be separated from your mirror lest a hair fall out of place or a speck of dirt land on your cheek!'

Kathryn turned her back, giving Jayne a target for her clenched fists.

'You may turn away, but it doesn't make any difference!' she cried, beating her sister's shoulders. 'I shall tell Father that each ruby set in gold which adorns your gown cost seven guineas, and that they are so numerously scattered he had best sell his entire flock of sheep to pay for them!'

'Liar!' Kathryn turned and stamped her feet. She seized Jayne's dark brown hair and pulled fiercely.

Mary watched in uneasy silence, knowing that to interfere would be to invite a vicious attack from both girls.

Soon they were tugging and wrestling, and falling to the floor, until Lady Anne entered and, finding them brawling, blamed John for the unruliness of his workshop. Such conduct gave the women in the workshop great scope for gossip.

'It's my belief that Jayne will one day choke on her own venom,' Marion announced as dusk fell.

'And Kathryn will explode in flames,' Bess added. 'Then all our fine work will be wasted, for there will be no one to wear the gowns at court.'

'Unless Mary and I took their places,' Marion mused. 'Now, Mary, what do you think of being decked out in rubies and presented to the Queen?'

'I should not like it,' Mary replied.

'What then of walking on Walter's arm, and having every lady in the land envy you?'

'Worse still!' She meant this with all her heart, for her own dreams were centred on the natural world of trees and flowers, neither did she aspire to making others jealous.

'Hah, John, you have bred a changeling child!' Marion turned to the master tailor brandishing her scissors as if to ward off strange spirits. 'She is like no other girl for primness and propriety!'

'And long may she continue as her precious self,' Bess put in. 'Mary is right to be suspicious. I for one would not ape the manners of the court, for the place is full of intrigue and deception!'

'And foolishness,' David Devereux muttered with a meaningful glance towards the window.

Out in the courtyard, Raleigh had returned from hunting with two London friends who had arrived at Saltleigh at his invitation. They were young men of not more than twenty, with thin beards and high voices, who laughed too readily at their friend's wit and drank too freely of Sir Sydney's strong beer.

'Come, Gresham, come, Harrington, leave your horses for the grooms!' Raleigh called. 'We must kick off our boots and find a roaring fire, for my fingers are frozen to the bone!'

So the visitors flung down the reins of their exhausted, lathered mounts, and, arm in arm, entered the house.

'One horse was badly lamed,' Hal told Mary later. 'He was Sir Sydney's favourite and will be sadly missed.'

The cousins sat in the empty workshop, with Mary still hard at work on the cloak. She was working a pattern of a snowflake out of silver thread, trying to achieve the feathery delicacy of the real thing. Each tiny stitch seemed to carry her lifeblood into the design, so intense was her absorption in the task.

'Honestly, child, I begin to think that you pour every ounce of your passionate nature into that work!' Bess had said to her earlier that day as she observed Mary secreted in her corner by the window. 'Your mind is lost in the curve of the silver thread and the sheen of velvet!'

'You hear me, Mary?' Hal said now. 'Sir Sydney's best hunter had to be destroyed.'

She looked up at last. ' 'Tis a shame.'

'Raleigh promises his father will send a horse from Hayes Barton, but Jeremy the cook says that the horses there are mere bags of bones in comparison.'

'I will be glad when they are all gone to court and the visit is over,' Mary said.

Hal agreed. 'Then there will be no more mountains of food to prepare or pots to wash, nor shadowy men in corridors, ready to kick out if you should happen to come across them when they are deep in secret conversation!'

Mary shot him a sharp glance. 'Which men? Do you mean this Gresham and Harrington?'

'No. The men I speak of come late at night and talk with Master Trevor. They give no names.'

Then Mary mentioned for the first time the close and feverish conversation that the steward had had in the workshop. 'I think they mean to bring Rome back into the English court,' she explained. 'They will do it in secret, and Raleigh is to help them, though I don't see why or how.'

Hal shook his head. ' 'Tis as much as I can do to keep out of the way of the kicks they aim at my shins,' he declared. 'As for their whisperings and their secrets, let others puzzle over them and content yourself with stitching pretty snowflakes!'

Mary fumed over Hal's last remark for a long time after her cousin had gone. How dare he belittle her with talk of pretty snowflakes, when her heart and soul went into the work? He would not call a master mason's carvings on the church roof merely 'pretty', she reasoned. Nor a painter's portrayal of the Last Supper above the altar. No; these would be praised and called beautiful, but Hal didn't understand such things.

She was thus out of humour when a boy from the stables tapped on the window with a message from the house.

'Master Raleigh bids Mistress Mary take her latest piece of work to the withdrawing room!'

Mary frowned. By this time she was well used to the nightly visit to the workshop from Raleigh, and was almost accustomed to his teasing way, which seemed to mean nothing but at the same time caused him mild amusement. But it was the first time she had received a summons to go up to the house. She went reluctantly, using the kitchen entrance and making her way along the dark corridors, up the winding oak stair to the upper floor.

From Kathryn's bedchamber Mary heard the voices of Lady Anne and her elder daughter: the mother scolding, the girl weeping and wailing. She hurried on beneath iron sconces carrying thick wax candles, along a vast gallery lined with paintings in heavy gold frames. The long, wide corridor was lined with oak panels and carpeted with Turkeywork rugs; signs of Sir Sydney's high standing in the Devonshire neighbourhood.

At the far end of the gallery she stopped and knocked on the carved door. There was a short wait before Raleigh himself flung it open and swept her inside. Mary had never in her life been inside the grand withdrawing room, with its elaborate plasterwork ceiling and huge hearth. A large tapestry showing deer in a flower-filled forest glade hung from the ceiling to keep out any night-time draughts and deep, padded settles were ranged by the side of the fire.

'Here is Mary!' Raleigh announced to his friends, Harrington and Gresham.

The two spindly young men lounging on the long seats looked her up and down. 'Even you, Raleigh, did not do her justice in your description,' Gresham drawled, while the other got up and walked full circle around her.

Mary found it hard to hold up her head under such scrutiny. 'The boy bade me bring my work, sir.'

'Yes; the work.' Hurriedly Raleigh took it from her and cast his eye over it. 'Snowflakes,' he murmured appreciatively.

Harrington whisked it from him. 'The maid's skill matches her beauty!' he crowed. 'My, what a clear, shining eye, what smooth, milky white skin!'

Now Mary's head went up, fierce and bold. Instinctively she sidestepped the drunken guest's attempt to encircle her waist with his arm, then retreated to the door.

'Do not frighten her with your lechery, Harrington!' Gresham remonstrated. 'Come here,' he told her more gently. 'We only wish to look at you, to judge whether you are indeed the fairest lady on this estate!'

Shocked, Mary managed to conceal a sharp gasp and remain silent.

'That is what Raleigh told us, and we wagered a guinea against it. But now I see we lose our wager, for the seamstress is worth three times the younger daughter and five times the elder!'

'Not to mention the mother,' Harrington laughed. 'Why, if they were to take her and burn her as a witch, I should not be out of humour for above ten seconds!'

The general laughter continued for enough time for

Mary to turn the door handle and slip out into the gallery. But she felt herself followed, and turned to see Raleigh pursuing her down the corridor.

'Pay them no heed,' he told her, striding ahead as they drew near to Lady Anne's bedchamber. 'They are students fresh from Oxford, whose pleasures lie in drinking, gambling and wenching. Indeed, Mary, I should not have paraded you before them, for they are unworthy of you!'

Mary bowed her head. An angry flush coloured her cheeks, while the candle flame cast long shadows from her thick eyelashes.

'Yes, I ought to have kept you to myself,' Raleigh murmured, handing back her work and looking thoughtful. 'Go now, child, and find your father. Ask him to take you home and keep you safe.'

Mary curtsied and hurried away, down the same stairs as before, her heart thumping. Only when she reached the cold air of the stable yard did the flames in her cheeks die down, yet by the time she entered her own workshop there were still tears in her eyes and the same pounding in her breast.

Be calm, she told herself, wishing now that she had never stayed behind while her father had ridden that afternoon to Plymouth to buy more cloth. He was due back soon, however, and even though the workshop was dark and empty, she decided to wait for him there, as planned, rather than risk the walk home alone.

She made her way as usual to her own quiet corner, taking advantage of the moonlight to find her stool and settle down to wait by the window. How beautiful the sky was, with its thin covering of silvery cloud and the mysterious moon almost full. She sighed and tried to shut out from her mind the encounter with Raleigh and his friends.

But her peace was soon broken by the click of the door latch and the low mutter of voices. For a moment, Mary thought Raleigh must have come to find her, so she shrank back into the corner, hoping that the deep shadows would conceal her presence. Then she heard Hugh Trevor speak.

'Quickly tell me: what news?' he urged the two men who accompanied him.

The answer came in a strange accent: 'Philip of Spain continues to build his Armada, the French court harbours many English families who stay faithful to Rome; all pray daily for the downfall of Elizabeth.'

'Yes, yes, but prayers alone will not accomplish it!' Trevor said impatiently. 'I mean, what news of plans closer to home?'

'There are many within the English court who work secretly on our behalf,' the second man informed him. 'But still no one succeeds in gaining the Queen's trust. We come to hear news of your man, Raleigh.'

'He is not my man,' the steward insisted, 'and my news is only that he stays here in preparation for the visit to

Greenwich, where he hopes to flatter his way back into favour.'

His answer angered the foreign-sounding man. 'We expected more. Remember that you are in our pay. We need something to show for our expenditure.'

'Be patient,' Trevor said. 'Return in January and you will hear that Raleigh has the Queen's ear and much more besides!'

As the three men drew closer and more secretive, Mary had to strain to hear. Leaning forward, she saw the door open a second time and the familiar figure of her father appear. She rose to warn him not to enter, but found that by doing this she would only betray her own presence. Besides, the plotters were so deeply involved in their conversation that they had not noticed the tailor's entrance.

'And when Raleigh succeeds in gaining favour, what then?' the foreigner asked. 'His heart is not for Rome; at least not to my knowledge.'

'His heart is for himself, and no man else,' Trevor assured him. 'Put reward in his way and he will snap it up. But he will cost you dear.'

The two men listened closely. 'How would a dukedom seem? And perhaps an estate in Oxford, together with rights to a settlement in the Americas.'

'They would sit prettily on his shoulders, I dare say.' Trevor's sly tone caused the others to smile.

'I trust you have your man's true measure,' the second stranger went on. 'Is he bold enough to carry out our deed: to kill the queen?'

John Devereux, who had halted in surprise by the door, now stifled an outraged cry. Mary's father stepped clear of the shadow of the door arch and impetuously spoke out.

'Sirs, I am no politician, but even to such a plain man as me your purpose is clear, and I challenge you upon your allegiance to come before Walter Raleigh and repeat what I have just heard!'

The startled men whirled round to face him.

' 'Tis the master tailor!' Trevor cried. 'He has heard from us what he ought not!'

Straight away the foreigner pulled a knife from under his cloak and lifted the blade to shoulder height.

'Hold your hand!' At first the steward tried to hold the man back, but then the second stranger drew a knife and moved in on John.

In her corner, Mary sat stock still with fear. Terror seized her and, though she longed to rise and spring forward, to stop the knife as it rose through the air and descended again, she was frozen, mute – as if made of stone.

She saw cloaks fly wide, heard feet scuffle, then all of a sudden someone cried out and fell to the ground.

'You have killed him!' Trevor gasped. 'Come away!'

Then, almost before the words were out of his mouth, the three men fled.

Mary ran from her hiding place and knelt beside her father. 'What have they done?' she gasped.

John tried to lift his head, but could only turn it towards her. 'Mary, my child!'

'Oh Father, where are you hurt?' Frantically she sought for his wound until her fingers found a place soaked with blood. It ran freely from his chest, pouring down his side and spreading on to the stone floor.

'Mary, these men have dealt me a fatal blow!' he moaned. 'Listen, child: tell no one of what you have seen here!'

'Hush!' she cried. 'You will not die!'

'As sure as there's a God in heaven, I shall,' he whispered. His eyelids flickered and he fought for breath. 'Promise me, Mary, that you will remain silent. Do not mention Trevor's name in this, else he will turn on you and have you killed!'

'Stay!' she pleaded. 'Do not leave me!' Alone. Without mother or father. 'Do not die!' she sobbed.

'Give me your promise and I will leave this world in peace. Mary; promise me!'

Desperately she kissed her father's cheek, then laid her own against his. 'I promise!'

John grasped her hand. He said no more, and soon his spirit slipped away.

Seven

It was as if time stood still. As if Mary's own breathing had stopped with her father's, and all the world had slipped from her, there in the darkness.

'Father,' she said in a broken voice.

He lay lifeless, his hand growing cold.

All was silent, except for the drumming of her heart against her ribs.

Then there were shadows at the window and the sound of the door opening once more. Still Mary did not move.

'Make haste!' a voice whispered.

Then a figure appeared brandishing a flaming torch, and instinctively Mary withdrew to her corner. The murderers had returned.

'Set the fire to the bolts of cloth!' the first said. 'They will burn well.'

The second laid the torch under the silks and taffetas which John had bought in Plymouth that afternoon. Mary saw the flames take hold of the fabric, and watched as the men rushed from place to place, lighting small fires wherever they could. The flames flickered at first, then licked harder at the piles of cloth, travelling swiftly and flaring high into the air.

'The deed is done!' the leader of the two men said at last, withdrawing to the door, where they laid the torch. Then they slipped out into the night.

'It seemed another age before Mary could move. She watched the flames take hold and illuminate her father's body, gathering strength as they ignited wooden chests and benches around. But all she could think of was her poor, dear father, stabbed to death in front of her eyes.

'Fire!' A startled cry from the courtyard roused her into action.

Quickly she ran and knelt at John's side. By this time smoke had filled the room, making her eyes smart. It filled her lungs, stifling and choking her. 'I will *not* leave you here!' she promised, seizing her father under the arms and trying to drag his body towards the already burning door. But he was heavy, and the smoke made her weak.

'Lord have mercy!' Helpless cries from the yard penetrated her consciousness. Then Lady Anne's rose above the rest, crying out instructions.

'Save the precious things! Bring out the court gowns and jewels, leave the rest if you must!'

Suddenly the door opened, and a gust of wind sent the flames roaring to the ceiling. Beyond the flames, many figures armed with blankets and pails of water were poised ready to enter.

'Make haste!' Lady Anne ordered.

But the flames were too fierce.

Mary tried to suck air into her lungs, but the hot smoke was everywhere. She must drag her father towards the window. Turning round, almost blinded, she used superhuman effort to move his body a little way across the stone floor.

Then there was a crack and the sound of glass splintering. Men tore at the leaded panes, making a gap large enough to climb through. They entered, their faces covered by cloths doused in water, fumbling through the smoke, finding their way towards the chests which contained the Campernowne family's half-finished court costumes.

And now the crackle and roar of flames deadened all other sounds, the smoke grew thick and black, and even the rafters in the roof began to blaze. In the unbearable heat, Mary was forced to let go of her father's body and slump to the floor.

Then hands grabbed her and pulled her upright. Almost senseless, still she felt herself swept into someone's arms and carried towards the window. She was lifted and passed to a rescuer waiting outside, felt the cold blast of winter air, gasped, saw the blur of David Devereux's features, then sank unconscious against his chest.

' 'Twas Hal that carried you from the flames,' Bess whispered.

Mary had opened her eyes to dim morning light, but where she was and what had happened she could not tell.

'But for him, you would have burned along with the workshop, which is mere cinders and ashes.' The kindly seamstress stroked Mary's face. 'Child, do you hear what I tell you?'

Mary nodded. She looked helplessly around the room, and discovered that she was in the servants' quarters above the stables, where Bess, Marion and the rest of the serving women nightly laid their heads.

'Do you know the fate of your poor father?' Bess asked gently.

Another nod, while tears appeared in Bess's eyes.

'They could not save him,' she explained. 'Oh, child, how could this happen?'

'Did they leave him to burn?' Mary's voice sounded hoarse and stumbling. She felt tears stream down her cheeks.

Bess raised her and softly rocked her. 'Poor orphan child,' she murmured. 'Do not fear, for I will be a mother to you as best I can. We will not let you starve.'

'Here, Mary; drink this clean water.' This time it was Marion's voice, full of concern and tenderness. 'Child, you must thank God and young Hal, for without them you would have perished.'

'Would that I had!' Mary cried bitterly. Both her father and her mother had been cruelly torn from her. There was no one in the world left to love.

'Let her weep,' Bess told Marion, 'for she has good cause.'

Many days passed before Mary's grief eased. Christmastide came and went in the rustle of Bess's wide kersey skirts and the heavy shuffle of her feet on rough boards. The seamstress tried in vain at first to persuade Mary to take food, only succeeding in making her drink plain water.

'Time will heal,' she assured the stricken girl. She saw to her every comfort, and gradually brought her back into the world of events beyond the servants' loft.

'Would you believe; her Ladyship sent Jeremy and Jack and every able-bodied man into the flames to bring out her gowns!' she would cluck and sigh. 'Sir Sydney would not have risked his cook for a mere pair of silk bodies, you may be sure.'

And then: 'Kathryn and Jayne complain the whole day through that they cannot now wear the partlets of worked roses at court, for they will not be ready in time. Their mother scolds and threatens not to take them to Greenwich, but the girls know full well that she would rather cut off her right arm than that they should forego the Queen's invitation. Meantime, Raleigh curses the entire household for leaving his cloak to perish in the flames.'

At this, Mary turned her head. 'Was none of the work on the panels saved?'

'None. And worse still: the patterns too were destroyed.' Bess had shrewdly judged that her words would rouse Mary from her week-long apathy. 'They say that none but your father knew the design.'

As Bess bathed her feverish face, Mary remained silent. 'They do not say true,' she confessed at last. 'I helped Father in the design of the cloak.'

'Indeed?'

'Yes. I recall every detail. It is impressed in my heart; every piece of the slipstitching and couched work, the pattern and colours, the style of the collar, the position of every last diamond set in gold.' It was true; for many days leading up to the fire Mary had done nothing but breathe, sleep and eat the working of the cloak.

'Yes, I believe it is so.' Bess nodded and stared thoughtfully at Mary. 'I wonder,' she murmured, then left unsaid what it was she was thinking of.

And the world outside went on at its usual pace, with only a visit from Hal to break the emptiness of Mary's feverish existence.

'It seems I must wear skirts and petticoats to enter here,' were his first words as he climbed the stepladder into the loft. Seizing a blanket, he held it around his waist and dropped a low curtsey.

Mary smiled, then burst into tears.

'Lord, is this the effect I have on the ladies!' Hal cried, casting off his disguise. 'No weeping and wailing, Mistress Mary; else I shall lose my manhood in earnest and howl alongside you!'

He sat at the edge of the bed and told her she looked thin and pale. 'I wager you weigh no more than a brace of sparrows together, but one of Jeremy's game pies would soon fatten you up, I'll be bound.'

Quickly Mary dried her tears. 'I owe you my life,' she said quietly.

He grinned back. 'Yes, and this is the thanks I earn; for you will not last out the week unless you take some food!'

'I cannot eat.'

'Why, 'tis only a matter of opening your mouth and pushing in one of these pieces of succulent roasted chicken,' he declared, producing a pewter salver and taking off the lid. 'There's nothing easier!'

Reluctantly, she took the food. 'Hal, have they buried my father?' she asked in a quavering voice, steeling herself for the reply.

'They have, though the ground was frozen almost solid. My own father said the prayers over his grave, while Sir Sydney himself attended and promised that you, Mary, shall have a roof over your head here at Saltleigh for as long as you wish.'

'I wish only to join my mother and father in the cold ground,' she said sadly.

Hal looked away. 'You shall in good time, mistress. So shall we all.' Sighing, he turned back and sought out her gaze. 'Meantime, we miserable wretches must crawl between heaven and hell, here on this barren earth.'

'Don't say so, Hal! You, above all people, should not have these gloomy thoughts.'

'Why me above all?'

'Because you are young and in good health, and have not suffered loss.'

'Have I not lost a mother, just as you did?' he reminded her. 'Fever took her the day I was born, and left my father to raise me.'

Mary humbly said sorry, then fell silent.

'Eat!' he encouraged. 'Regain your strength, and pray for your father's soul in heaven.'

'I will,' she promised, from that time forth determined to look ahead as best she could.

The New Year broke clear and bright, with Mary now well enough to venture from her bed into the frosty sunlight. She took her first steps out of doors on Bess's arm, able to look up at the blue sky and the rooks cawing from the tall elm trees that formed a shield for the hall against the high winds from the sea.

Less welcome was her first sight of the burned out workshop. She looked in dread at the black spars of the upright wooden shafts which had supported the walls, and at the tumbled rafters lying criss-crossed across the stone floor. Of the windows and door, nothing remained.

'Come away,' Bess urged, leading her a few steps along the drive away from the house.

In the distance, Mary saw Sir Sydney and Raleigh riding over the crest of a hill with dogs running at their side; colourful figures dressed in scarlet, green and black, with fine feathers in their beaver hats.

'Raleigh has searched high and low for a master tailor who will make him a cloak,' Bess remarked. 'But creditors are gnawing at his heels, and members of the guild know it. Before the fire he was relying on Sir Sydney's generosity, and still continues to do so. He even came to your Uncle David and begged on bended knee for him to take up the work. But David told him he had not the skill.'

Mary said nothing, except that her legs were weak and she could go no further. So they turned, hearing the men gallop up behind them.

'Aha, 'tis the little seamstress!' Raleigh cried heartily as he passed by. He charged into the courtyard, dismounted, then flung his reins at the nearest bystander, who happened to be Hugh Trevor, the stiff, sober-suited steward.

Sir Sydney reined back his horse. 'Mary, I am sorry for your loss. Your father was a good man and true. However, I am glad to see you grow stronger. Now, take fair warning: my wife wishes to talk with you as soon as you are able,' he told her.

She curtsied and kept her gaze low.

'Don't be afraid, child. Her Ladyship knows you are grieving for your father; God willing, she will not treat you harshly. Come this night after supper to the great gallery. Wait there and she will come.'

Another curtsey satisfied him and he rode on.

Bess felt Mary's frail figure start to tremble. 'Come into the kitchens where it is warm,' she murmured. 'Jeremy will give you honey and spices mixed in hot water to restore your spirits.'

In they went, to the hurly-burly of clashing pots, clattering knives and sharp orders yelled along dark corridors; to the splash of water and the bubble of kettles, the thump of pastry against boards and the rising of bread in the hearth.

'Why, mistress, you are back from the dead!' Jack the potboy cried, scuttling by with a wooden ladle. ' 'Tis the ghost of Mistress Mary!' he told the others, until Hal stopped his mouth with a quick box around the ears.

'You are still shaking!' Bess declared as she sat Mary by the fire. 'What is the matter, child?'

Mary shook her head and tried to calm herself. 'Her Ladyship will ask me about the fire,' she whispered.

'Only to discover what you recall of events leading up to it.' Bess held her by the hand, crouching down beside her. 'It is natural that she should. You must make quick answers and get it over with; the sooner the better.'

But Mary's trembling only increased. 'I cannot!'

'Yes, child, you must.'

'I cannot!' she repeated. All at once the flames roared again in her ears, and her father's dying words came sighing through: 'Tell no one what you have seen here!'

'Then say as much as you are able,' Bess told her kindly. Lord knew what horror the poor girl had witnessed. 'Sir Sydney will understand.'

Mary stood waiting under a portrait of Sir Christopher Campernowne, Sir Sydney's father. The canvas loomed over her in its heavy gilt frame, its dark background creating a gloomy effect. Sir Christopher's hand rested on a human skull, which sat on a table in the foreground, beside a silver plate. He wore a long black velvet gown with a sable collar over a rich red doublet, and a heavy chain of office hung around his neck. His face was severe, and the skull gave the portrait an eerie feel.

'Do you know what this signifies, child?'

A voice at Mary's shoulder made her jump and turn to see Raleigh standing at her shoulder and pointing at the death's head.

'No sir.'

' 'Tis a *memento mori*, a reminder of our mortality. In spite of our wealth and power, we must all turn to dust.'

Mary shuddered and moved away.

'Ah yes, I forgot. You need no reminder.' More serious than usual, Raleigh wandered on down the gallery into the withdrawing room.

Soon Lady Anne emerged from her bedchamber. Spying Mary, she drew her into a window seat beneath one of the tall windows and began her inquisition. 'What was the cause of this great fire?' she demanded.

Mary took a deep breath. 'I do not know, my Lady.' Pray God will preserve my wicked, untruthful soul! she implored silently.

'But you were there, within the workshop. Surely you saw the flames start up?'

Pinned against the cold window panes, Mary shook her head.

'Come, come, don't play the fool with me. Were you alone with your father? Did a candle overturn and set fire to a piece of work? Were your backs turned? Did anyone try to raise the alarm?'

'I don't know. I was not there at the start.' The lies tumbled clumsily from Mary's lips as she saw Sir Sydney approach down the long gallery with his steward.

'Wife, do not be so harsh. The girl trembles, do you not see?'

Lady Anne stood up and replied stiffly. 'Husband, I merely wish to discover the cause of the blaze. It may be that the child holds the answers.'

'And perhaps the full reason will never come to light,'

Sir Sydney replied. 'Master Trevor here was in the courtyard tending to some business when the cry went up. He tells me that he ran to a window near to the door and saw that a candle had fallen from an iron bracket on to a wooden chest piled high with cloth and that the flames had already taken hold.'

Stealing a look at the steward, Mary noted that his face was set in firm lines, his chin jutting out slightly, his eyes focused on the distant end of the corridor.

Her husband's information made Lady Anne pause. Then she turned back to Mary. 'Then you were inside the room when the blaze started; how else could you have got in, since it began near to the door?'

'I don't remember, my Lady!'

'Do not, or *will* not!' Lady Anne said, angrily taking Mary by the wrist. 'You are a clumsy girl, are you not; a girl who would knock over a candle and start a fire? And a dishonest one who would conceal the truth to save herself!'

Mary closed her eyes to shut out the sight of the traitor, Hugh Trevor, his expression blank, his shoulders drawn back as he stood to attention by Sir Sydney's side. 'I came later!' she insisted. 'I found my father lying in the midst of the flames. I could not save him!' There was a deadly secret that could not be told. 'On my own life, my Lady, I would have given my last breath to have saved him!'

'Wife, have done!' Sir Sydney insisted as Mary began to sob.

'No, I will not.' Lady Anne dragged Mary down the gallery. 'Come, girl. Tomorrow I will set you to work on Jayne's court gown, for now I am sure that you are partly to blame, and you may shed tears 'til Kingdom come, still I will not soften my resolve!'

Sir Sydney followed them, closely shadowed by Trevor. 'Hold your hand! The child ails. She cannot work.'

Lady Anne turned sharply. 'Husband, you must give me leave to treat the girl as I choose. I am a better judge of her nature than you. Tend to your hounds and let me deal with Mistress Mary!'

At that moment, the door of the withdrawing chamber opened and Raleigh came out. He stood between Mary and Lady Anne, seizing her Ladyship's hand and unclasping the fingers from around Mary's wrist. 'I would treat my dog better than you treat this child,' he muttered, silencing her with a fierce glare. Then he smoothed the anger from his brow and turned to Sir Sydney.

'Uncle,' he began, 'I see here a solution to the most pressing problem of my cloak!'

'You do?' Sir Sydney frowned. His wife had once again achieved the difficult task of putting him quite out of temper.

'Indeed, sir. Your seamstress, Bess, confides in me that Mistress Mary is no mere plain sewer of cambric shifts like most girls of her age, but a needlewoman skilled beyond her years. And to be frank, I have noted her work with some wonder and admiration. Why, one evening I called her to the house to show her couched work to Gresham and—'

'Yes, yes, nephew. What of it?'

'The fact is, sir, that Bess tells me that Mary holds in her memory the very pattern to my cloak! Don't you see? Here is the girl who can take up the task which her father began.'

Raleigh's suave suggestion swept Lady Anne into a fresh rage. 'There is Jayne's gown to finish, and Kathryn's head-dress! I will set the girl to my *own* work before our carousing, good for nothing nephew's!'

'I will put her here in the withdrawing room, sir, with velvet and threads.' Raleigh ignored the outburst and went on with his plan for Mary. 'You see how weak she is. The attic rooms where the tailors now work are too cold and bare.'

Sir Sydney listened, looked at Mary, then nodded. 'As you wish, Walter. But don't work the girl to death on the one hand, nor fill her head with foolish vanities on the other.'

'Husband!' Lady Anne stormed, clenching her fists and pressing them against her mouth. 'You know nothing of the work still to be done for our daughters!'

Sir Sydney turned to face her, as if all his life he had built up to this moment of truth. His face grew red and flecks of spittle appeared on his lips. 'I know one thing, wife. I have long lived to rue the day when I married you, for you are a vinegar-faced shrew whose selfishness defies belief. And take heed; for your daughters, Mistress, are fast following in their mother's footsteps!'

With this, he gave a slight bow, turned and went.

'Come, Mary,' Raleigh said, offering her his hand. He swept past Trevor and Lady Anne, leading her after Sir Sydney. 'You will make me a cloak. I will wear it at Greenwich. And praise for your work will be on the lips of all the Queen's courtiers, and the Queen herself will commend it!'

Eight

There was much gossip in the kitchens and attics of Saltleigh Hall.

'Her Ladyship will not stay in the same room with her husband since the falling out over Raleigh's cloak,' Marion would whisper to her nearest neighbour, careless of the watchful eye of David Devereux. 'Neither will she perform her wifely duties, if the word of her Italian maidservant is to be believed.'

Bess overheard this tidbit many times and at last took it upon herself to beard Sophia in her den. She had called at Lady Anne's bedchamber to leave a pair of kid leather gloves adorned with gold, to be worn by her Ladyship at Greenwich, when she found Sophia alone there.

'How does your mistress?' the seamstress asked boldly, woman to woman. 'They say that she is constantly in an ill humour and none dare cross her path.'

Sophia looked down her nose. 'Far be it from me to chitter chatter on such matters, mistress, for whatever I say is taken and trumpeted to the world at large.'

'Yes, yes, your Italian airs and graces are very fine, but I pity you if what they say is true: that Sir Sydney rues the day he married Lady Anne and has left her in no doubt over it, and that he spends his days with his dogs, whom he regards as better company by far than that of his lady wife!'

Sighing, Sophia laid fresh linen inside an oak chest by the window. 'I cannot deny it. And so my mistress rails against men and poisons her daughters with her views. She tells them that women outstrip men in intellect and ability; that it must be so, for your sovereign queen is living proof.'

'Thus far I will agree,' Bess said with a merry laugh. 'My three husbands have proved to be weak and ailing creatures who chose to expire rather than face the responsibility of a wife and family!'

Sophia smiled at this. 'I must choose my husbands more wisely then.'

'They say that your Italians make passionate lovers,' Bess said enviously. 'While your Englishman is reserved.'

'Not all,' Sophia countered. 'Walter Raleigh would prove as loving as any of my countrymen, I'll be bound!'

'Evidence, mistress!' Bess clamoured, eager for more tasty tidbits.

But Sophia blushed prettily and retreated to the inner chamber. 'I will show Lady Anne these gloves!' she called, as Jayne and Kathryn burst suddenly into their mother's chamber.

'What are you doing out of the attic?' Kathryn demanded of Bess, whose deep curtsey had failed to soothe the girl's irritation. 'Get back to work, else the court outfits will never be ready!'

Bess withdrew without protest and, after discovering from Sophia that their mother was gone to town, the two daughters rushed on to the withdrawing chamber specially to torment Mary.

'See how she sits hunched over her work!' Jayne began, finding her immersed in a border of silver latticework. 'You must chide her, Kathryn, for not setting her cap properly on her head, and for forgetting to curtsey as we came into the room!'

The older girl went and pinched Mary's arm. 'There! And there!' She tugged at the cap to expose Mary's coiled braids. 'Don't think that because our cousin favours you, you are like to remain here at Saltleigh after he is gone!'

'No, for we are set on your leaving, and we will tell Mother so. She will not want you here either, for you have lied to her about the fire!'

Mary tried hard not to react, though the darts of the girls' spite were sharp. She stared intently at the small dish of silver spangles which she was using to decorate the lattice border, thinking that they little suspected how big was the lie she must conceal.

'Besides, we know why Walter has made you his favourite!' Kathryn sniggered. 'He has a roving eye, and there is no wench too young nor too lowly to catch it!'

A sharp intake of breath from Mary showed the struggle she was having to keep quiet.

'No; nor too plain and ignorant!' Jayne cried. 'Look at her ugly dark hair, Sister. Did you ever see the like? And all she knows is needlework. Music and dancing mean nothing to her!'

Kathryn studied Mary, resenting the glaring fact that there was grace and finesse in her fingers as she drew the thread through the velvet, that the hair unfurling down her back was thick and glossy and that her features were delicate and even. 'What need does a pauper have of music?' she sneered.

'Or of dancing!' Jayne echoed, lifting her skirts and raising herself on tiptoe to perform a little jig. 'Think of us at Greenwich, Mistress Mary, with the lutes playing and the court gentlemen asking us to dance. And we will think of you on the streets of Plymouth in the cold, cold snow, with no roof over your head and no food in your belly!'

Laughing, she and Kathryn twirled and dipped, tapped their toes and kicked their heels.

'Picture that!' Kathryn cried, as they danced out of the room.

Mary sighed and sat up straight to ease her back and neck. She had grown used to the petty threats, but the idea that Raleigh favoured her for reasons other than her skill with the needle worried her.

I am yet thirteen, she reminded herself, with no father or mother to guide me. Bess is of no use here, for she would marry me to the next shepherd who passed by the door, and within a year this maid would be a mother. Likewise Marion. Nor can I go to Hal for advice; he knows as little of the world as I do, and besides he would laugh at the very idea.

The problem stayed with her, even when she resumed her chain stitch, until Hal broke in with a message from Raleigh.

'Good morrow, my Lady!' he began, bowing low. 'Might I speak with your Ladyship? Pray lend an ear to your humble servant!'

'Hal, leave off your foolishness!' she grinned. 'Or rather, if you will: smooth your hair and straighten your doublet before you address me, for I am very grand now, as you see, and will not speak with ragamuffins!'

'Oh Lord!' Hal crowed. 'Mistress Mary has risen high from her common beginnings; 'tis as I suspected! She sits in comfort beside a warm fire, 'neath tapestries and candles, amidst great daintiness. How then shall I address her?'

'Give me your message and be on your way,' she told him.

'Oh, your Ladyship, no! I may not bother your brains with this and that, for I do see you are too grand and I am too low!'

'Hal, *tell* me!'

'No, indeed. Well, 'tis only that the rogue and adventurer, that roisterer, Walter Raleigh, sends word that his friend, Gresham, is returning to Saltleigh this very night with his groom and manservant.'

'Hush, Hal!' Mary warned, looking anxiously around.

'Is it "hush!", or is it, "tell me!"?'

'Both,' Mary told him, ending the foolishness. 'What is it to me that Gresham comes here?'

'The gentlemen will gather here in this room, and Raleigh says you must depart, back to the attic with Bess and Marion.'

'And that is all?'

Hal winked. 'No more my Ladyships, at least for a time.'

'And I am glad of it,' she said.

Mary thought more on this after her cousin had left, and found herself surprisingly reluctant to leave the Turkey rugs and the fine hangings behind. She liked to look at the tapestries, picking out the story of the nobleman and his men hunting the stag in the tall forest, with the roe deer gathered in a clearing to one side, and the ladies picking flowers and playing the harp to the other. She imagined herself a damsel in those far off days, wearing a close-fitting gown and a low girdle, her plaited hair swinging at her slender waist, gathering daisies. There would be a knight on a white horse, his armour glittering in the dappled sunlight. All would be natural and innocent.

She shook herself and took up her work. She gave herself to the straight lines and curves, to the spangles and seed pearls, the delicate flowers and all the images of nature that she and her father had designed for the cloak. She would depict the stars of the heavens, the wind in the trees; she would perfect them and for his dear sake produce such a work as had never been seen!

By night Mary lived the life of any other servant: eating in the kitchens, laying her head on a straw mattress in the loft. But by day, when the other seamstresses climbed the narrow steps to the dusty attics, Mary was called back to the withdrawing chamber to sit at her work.

'Pay us no attention, child,' Raleigh said, the day after his visitor had returned. 'And if you sit quiet as a mouse, making no noise, we will not notice you.'

His friend, Gresham, smiled knowingly when Mary tried to resist. 'I hear you have survived the blaze in the workshop. Surely then you can survive the damp squibs of *our* idle chatter!'

They closed the door behind her, stoked the fire against the snowstorm outside, then sprawled on the cushioned settles.

'I have taken my father's house, close to the city,' Gresham told Raleigh with evident pride. 'He stays with my mother on his estate in Leicestershire, afflicted by the gout and unable to travel. But for me, the house would stand empty.'

Raleigh affected not to be impressed. 'A house close to the city is neither one thing nor another. It lacks the advantage of the country, without the convenience of the town.'

Gresham got up to toss him an apple from the carved platter on the window-sill near to where Mary sat. 'You will not say so when I tell you where it is.'

A knock at the door interrupted the conversation. Gresham, who was still on his feet, answered it. ' 'Tis the stiff and sober steward,' he reported. 'Shall I send him away, or shall we have some entertainment at his expense?'

'The latter,' Raleigh decided, to Mary's dismay.

Trevor entered and stated his business. 'I must make an inventory for Sir Sydney of all the jewels to be used in the making of the court gowns,' he informed them. 'Both here and in the workshop.'

'Aha!' Gresham seized Raleigh and pulled him to his feet. 'Your uncle keeps account of your extravagance at last!'

'What do I care?' Raleigh shrugged. 'Count away,' he told Trevor, 'but don't frighten the girl with your poker face!'

Mary held her breath as Trevor approached and took up the dish of seed pearls which she was sewing into the collar of the cloak. His close presence almost stifled her; the sour stench of his breath on her face turned her stomach.

'See, she goes pale,' Raleigh pointed out. 'You have no way with the ladies I see, steward!'

'Aye, poor orphan child,' Trevor murmured, still steadily counting. 'She has grown thin since her father's death, and no wonder.'

'Lord, the man has feelings after all!' Raleigh said with disbelief. 'Why, I thought you were made of stone!'

'By no means,' Trevor protested. 'My calling is to serve without question, but I am a man with many sympathies, like any other.' To show his sincerity, he smiled at Mary and laid his hand upon her head. She tried hard to bear his touch without flinching.

'Ha, the steward shows us his softer side!' Gresham declared. 'The world is full of wonders!'

'I wish you well, sirs, though you joke at my expense. Young gentlemen of learning and taste are always to be admired.'

'Does he flatter us, Gresham?'

'I think he does, Raleigh!'

' 'Tis no flattery,' Trevor assured them, turning first to Gresham and then to Raleigh. 'I know your reputations: yours as a scholar, sir, and yours as a soldier, sailor and loyal friend to our great Queen.'

Raleigh inclined his head. 'Loyal, to be sure. Above all, loyal.'

There was a silence, then Trevor grew bolder. 'Fear not, sir. Though fortunes and fashions change by the day, loyalty endures. It rises to the surface, like cream on the milk, and it is noticed by those on high.'

'Perhaps,' Raleigh muttered uncertainly.

Gresham stepped in to encourage his friend. 'Come, Walter, the Queen knows your name at least. As for me, she would not recognise me from Adam.'

'But my name is soiled in her eyes,' Raleigh pointed out. 'I have much work to do to restore it.'

'For shame, sir,' Trevor cut in. 'You have sailed the ocean for her and fought in Ireland. The Queen will not forget.'

'Yes, Walter. You must practise your poetry and perfect your jig,' Gresham urged. 'Oh, and by the bye, did I mention that my father's house stands by the river in Greenwich?'

The news stopped Raleigh in his tracks. Then he laughed and slapped his friend on the back. 'You hear that, steward? Now I may take myself off and prepare myself for the Queen's visit in Greenwich, instead of rotting unseen, here in Devon!'

'Good fortune smiles on you,' Trevor replied. 'I wish you God speed, and hope that you may remember me when you are grown great and decked with the rewards you deserve.'

Bowing, Trevor backed out of the room to laughter from Gresham.

'A bold fellow!' he remarked.

'And ambitious,' Raleigh noted. The steward's flattery had worked on him a little. 'I will write him down as discreet and quick-witted; qualities not to be ignored.'

And untrustworthy! Mary's whole desire was to stand and unveil Trevor's wickedness. He talks of Rome, and plots against you and the Queen! The throne of England is in danger! Words tumbled through her mind, but she could not utter them.

She must not, for fear of her own life. And because she had given her promise to her father. Her head spinning, her chest constricted, Mary tried to stand. Instead, she swayed and leaned against the sill.

'The child faints!' Gresham cried, rushing to her aid.

But Raleigh was there first, supporting Mary and carrying her to the settle. 'Bring Bess from the workroom,' he said. 'She will look after her and restore her wits!'

'There is nothing the matter that time will not heal,' Bess insisted to David. 'Pity the poor girl in that stifling chamber, deprived of our company, forced to listen to the foolishness of two vain young men, the butt of any savagery that Mistress Jayne and Mistress Kathryn care to inflict! What wonder then that she faints and has to be carried into our care!'

Mary had come to in the long, low attic. Gradually she had made out the snip of shears into cloth and the low chatter of people working. Then her eyes had focused on the benches, and on her uncle sitting cross-legged on a low platform at the head of the room. Marion had seen her first movements and quickly run to tend to her.

'Drink this,' she instructed, holding cold water to Mary's lips. She looked troubled, and Mary soon learned the reason why.

' 'Tis a great pity that Sir Sydney cannot trust us!' Bess was saying to Hugh Trevor, who stalked up and down the rows of benches. 'What need is there of your inventory when we work loyally and without complaint?'

'This is the work of her Ladyship,' Marion grumbled to Mary. 'She wishes to show up her nephew for his extravagance and prove to Sir Sydney that he is a fool to send him to Greenwich!'

Slowly Mary sat up to follow events.

'Fifty-two rubies, twenty-seven diamonds, two hundred and fifty emeralds . . .' Trevor read from a long list, trying to account for each precious item. 'As for your pearls, I have counted five hundred and ten, but there is record of ten more still missing.' The steward came to a halt by David's platform. 'Can you explain, sir, why ten of the largest and most perfect pearls have disappeared?'

David shook his head. 'I cannot, Master Trevor. There has been such turmoil since the workshop was burned, that I can only guess that they were lost in the fire.'

'Good reasoning, Devereux; but that I counted the gems

myself the day *after* the blaze, and by my reckoning there were five hundred and twenty pearls of assorted quality here in this leather pouch.' Trevor held up the bag with a dark look. 'Who will find me these ten missing pearls?' he demanded. 'Speak now.'

There was a low muttering and many worried frowns, but no one came forward.

Mary stared at the stern black figure who had so lately fawned over Raleigh. What was to stop him, she wondered, from secreting the pearls himself, or from selling them on to a jewel merchant in Plymouth? The man was not beyond thus deceitfully lining his own pockets.

'If none admits it, then I will search this house from cellar to attic!' the steward warned.

'Yes, and blame some poor innocent for his own carelessness,' Marion murmured.

'Or worse!' Mary whispered. It was as much as she dared say.

Marion narrowed her eyes and stared at Trevor. 'I never did like the man,' she declared, 'but now it goes beyond that.'

'What do you mean?' Mary leaned in towards the seamstress so that no one could overhear.

'I mistrust him!' Marion decided. 'He has a sly, mean look.'

By now, the steward had turned on his heel and was marching out of the attic. 'Take heed: I will find the missing pearls *and* the culprit!' he shot over his shoulder. At the last moment before he left, his eye fell on Mary. 'And I will punish her,' he said quietly, as if all his venom were poured into the one word, 'punish'.

Instinctively, Marion put her arm around Mary's shoulder.

'Or him,' Trevor went on. 'Lord knows, deceit is an evil which must be stamped on. Be it in high or low places, this dishonesty will be rooted out. It will be purged as a disease is bled by the physician, until the body of Saltleigh is restored to health!'

'And may God ensure that it is so,' Marion breathed. 'For we are all under the shadow of suspicion, and none may rest safe in their beds until the truth be told.'

Nine

To all at Sir Sydney Campernowne's estate, the New Year of 1582 had been rung in with disastrous consequences. It was as if the December fire had destroyed the sense of security and contentment which had long been part of the place: one season melting into the next, swallows nesting in the spring, raising their chicks and flying south, trees bursting their buds and spreading green shade against the summer sun, then blushing fiery orange and red before shedding crisp brown leaves on to the bare earth.

This January there was a fear creeping like mist through the workshops and stables, into the vaulted kitchens as the stern steward sought out the thief in their midst.

'Hugh Trevor be hanged!' Jeremy complained in his steaming kitchen. 'For there never was such a sneaking, creeping, overbearing man in all England!'

He slammed his cleaver into a haunch of venison, thumping the blade into the thick wooden block so that Jack the potboy jumped in the air.

'Is he the King of all Devon, that he must overturn every corner and cry thief into my very ovens? No, for he is as low as the rest of us, only dressed up like some jackanapes in a black doublet and stiff lace collar, parading his empty authority.'

Down came the cleaver through the raw meat, so that poor Jack shuddered at the cook's fat fingers and broad hands, imagining what minced work he would make of Trevor if he came across him on a dark night.

'He has left off poking through the flour bins,' Hal reported with a worried frown, 'and has hastened to see Lady Anne.'

'I had rather have rats scuttling in my cellars than that scoundrel!' Jeremy grumbled, tossing the meat into a sizzling kettle and crumbling salt into it. 'The devil take him!'

It was not long before the steward and the lady of the house descended once more into Jeremy's kingdom.

'Bring the potboy to me!' Lady Anne announced.

Jack was produced, quaking and cowering away from his grand mistress.

In front of the gathered crowd of kitchen workers, Lady Anne held up a creamy, glowing pearl between her thumb and forefinger. 'Explain to me, boy, how this and nine others were found tied inside your kerchief in the grain store.'

There was a gasp as Jack shook his head and straight away tried to dodge from the room.

'See how the guilty boy starts and runs!' Trevor said sourly.

Two men at the front of the group caught hold of the runaway and dragged him forward.

'What have you to say, sirrah?' The steward advanced and took the boy roughly by the throat. When Jack remained silent, like a rabbit caught in the glare of torchlight, he shook him and landed him a blow with his fist.

Jeremy growled and took a step forward, but it was Hal who jumped in to Jack's defence. 'This is no proof!' he cried. ' 'Tis a common kerchief, made from cut-offs from the tailors' basket. Who can say whether it truly belongs to Jack?'

At this Trevor released the boy and turned on his defender. 'Master Hal, is it?'

'Yes, Hal!' Jack's words spluttered into the awed silence. He'd found his voice at last and made all use of it he could to squeeze himself out of trouble. 'Hal is the one you seek, for I saw him yesternight skulking in the grain store!'

The mistress of Saltleigh seized on this. 'Hal Devereux, defend yourself!'

Hal raised himself up in indignation. 'I care not for this charge. 'Tis like a shotgun full of pellets, aimed into a crowd and fired. He who is hit by chance is called thief and taken to the gallows!'

'Proud, insolent boy . . .' Lady Anne began.

'Clever beyond his station,' Trevor added. 'This is the very boy who would steal and cheat, my Lady, and we have a witness in the potboy to prove the matter!'

113

Lady Anne turned back to Jack. 'Will you stand before the constable and swear in the eyes of God that what you say is true?' she demanded.

Shuddering and nodding, his eyes staring as if the noose were tightening on his very own neck, the boy swore that he would.

Then Hal, realising the danger of his own situation, decided to make himself scarce. He darted into the crowd, pushing his way through, and this time no hand was raised to prevent him.

'Stop him, fools!' Trevor cried, lunging after Hal. But several stout bodies blocked his way and gave Hal time to make good his escape.

Counting on the delay, Hal sped through the dark corridors, down back alleys and up stone steps into the daylight. His first instinct was to head for the attics and claim his father's protection, but he soon reasoned that this would make things worse. Trevor would pursue him there and draw David into the false accusation. So he skirted round the house, climbed a high stone wall into the vegetable garden, and from there slipped through a wooden gate into the fields beyond.

Meanwhile, Hugh Trevor made his way to the roof of the hall and to the flat, castellated terrace there. It was the best lookout point from which to see the surrounding countryside, with a view of the rolling hills and a glimpse of the iron grey sea in the distance. He climbed the spiral stairs in time to catch sight of a small figure fleeing into a copse of elms beyond the vegetable garden. With hooded eyes and a nod of satisfaction he noted that Hal had fled towards Plymouth, where he would no doubt lie low.

His aim to conceal the pearls and heighten suspicion at the Hall had succeeded. In fact, it had found an ideal target in Hal; better than he might have hoped. For Hal was Mary's cousin and he could now sow the seed in exactly the place he had first desired: with the little seamstress herself. The indirect route was always the best; it covered trails and left the perpetrator free of suspicion.

The girl has wormed herself into the heart of things, he told himself. Raleigh favours her and depends on her for the cloak. Hence I cannot move against her this week or next. Yet she may be a danger, for how much she understands of the fire and the cause of her father's death is unknown to me.

Trevor stayed at his lookout point long after Hal had disappeared, considering events with hooded eyes. His steaming breath billowed into the frosty air. She is a closed book, he thought; ever sly and secretive. But still I have made my first move. And when Raleigh is done with her, I shall link her with this so-called theft by accusing her of providing Hal with the kerchief made of scraps from the workshop. Her Ladyship is already ill-disposed towards her. How easy then to accuse her along with her cousin and send them both into the tight embrace of the hangman's noose!

'Hal will go to sea on the first ship he finds.' Marion spoke in a hushed voice in the still of the dark servants' loft. 'Never fear, Mary; they will not clap him in irons!'

'Poor David's heart is broke,' Bess sighed. 'Yet he will not show it, nor share his grief.'

'Lord knows if he will ever see his son again,' another said. 'It's my belief the Devereux family is cursed and that we should call in the priest to exorcise the devils that beleaguer it.'

'Hush, Joan!' came the warning from Bess. 'We want no talk of the devil here.'

Mary lay on her back, listening without reacting. She felt the sudden loss of her dear cousin more than she could say. Her heart was so full of woe that she thought it must break.

'Aye, to sea,' Marion whispered. 'With a new name towards a New World, and good riddance to the old one, which is rotten to the core!'

An ocean stretched before Mary in her mind's eye. The swelling of waves and the gusting of winds on a stormy sea. And she had not said goodbye, nor wished him well. She had not told him that she believed in his honesty and courage.

So she came to a decision and waited until the room fell silent, except for the even breathing of many sleeping forms. Then she raised herself up and made sure that none was awake, sliding then from the bed and slipping into her clothes without a single sound. Barefoot she crept from the room, down the ladder into the stable, where she found the horse named Heather, saddled and bridled her and led her into the yard.

Now every jingle of the horse's bridle and clip of her hooves sounded to Mary like trumpets announcing her departure. She held her breath and climbed the mounting block, slid into the saddle and eased Heather forward. No light appeared in either house or stables as she made her exit.

Thanking the Lord for sound sleepers, Mary soon reached the soft grass at the side of the lane, where she picked up speed, towards the empty cottage where she had lived with her mother and father. The cottage held many memories linking her to the past; it seemed every inch of its rough wattle walls spoke to her in the moonlight, and voices whispered in the air. Her old life, old voices; the ones she held dear.

And she remembered that her father's last thought had been for her. Tell no one, keep yourself safe, and I will go to my maker in peace. He rested now in a quiet grave. His soul was with God.

Her eyes were blurred with tears as she passed by the silent cottage. But she pressed on for town, welcoming the salt smells on the wind as she crossed fields, relying on the starlight and Heather's familiarity with the route.

Once clear of Sir Sydney's estate, and not wanting to arrive in town at the dead of night, Mary stopped by a sheep fold, took poor shelter by the low wall and waited for first light. Then, frozen almost to the core, she remounted her horse and travelled on.

By dawn, which arrived with a pink glow, they were within sight of Plymouth. The town, like the countryside around it, was covered with a thin layer of frozen snow, no longer pure white, but muddied and spoiled by cart tracks and the tramp of human feet. And Mary was surprised by the early bustle of the streets. Though barely daylight, they were busy with fish mongers returning from the harbour with their day's purchases, and by farmers' wives arriving early for market. There was much shouting and greeting, sometimes an argument, and here and there the sight of a homeless beggar hunched on a street corner, craving alms.

Mary hurried on towards the quayside, under the overhanging balconies of the houses and past the shuttered windows of the merchants. She prayed that Marion had guessed right about Hal's intention to go to sea, agreeing in her own mind that it was his best alternative, for the shadow of the gallows was a tall one, stretching the length and breadth of England.

'Now, mistress, what's your business?' people would ask her, stopping at their tasks of hoisting baskets of fish on to their shoulders or setting out their winter crops for sale.

Mary would shake her head and pass by, judging it

dangerous to mention Hal's name to all and sundry. Only when she gained a sight of the tall ships in the harbour did she dismount and begin to ask cautious questions of the sailors on the quay.

'A country lad, you say?' one old seaman replied. 'Bless you, maid; such boys come ten a penny every day of the year. You have beggars and thieves by the score, all desperate to leave these shores and strike out for a new life.'

'The boy I seek is neither beggar nor thief!' Mary insisted. 'He is my cousin, fallen on hard times through no fault of his own. He is tall and skinny, with dark eyes and reddish hair, with the earth of the country still on his shoes.'

'Then go seek him at the harbourmaster's house,' the kindly sailor told her. 'The captains of the tall ships gather there each morning to take on crew.'

Mary thanked him and hurriedly followed his advice.

At a tall, timbered house by the waterside she did indeed come across a number of weathered, rough-bearded men who turned out to be the captains of the ships anchored at the harbour's mouth. With a rapidly beating heart, she approached them one by one and mentioned Hal's name.

No, came the reply, often off-hand, sometimes amused by Mary's earnestness.

'Has he gone off and left you in the lurch?' one asked, guessing that the course of young love had not run smooth.

Mary tossed her head and walked away, not dignifying the question with a reply.

Then at last she came to a more important-looking man in well-tailored, russet doublet and hose. 'Sir, I am seeking Hal Devereux, late of Saltleigh Hall, for the purpose of bidding him farewell and good fortune.'

The man listened and was about to dismiss her, then he thought again. 'Give an account of the lad,' he invited. 'For though I know of none such, 'tis possible I misheard the name of one of the hands I will take on board today.'

Again Mary gave the description of Hal.

'There is one with that look,' the captain admitted. 'He goes by the name of Christopher Oak, though to my mind he seems more like a sapling than the fully-grown tree! Still, he will take up little space and serve well as cabin boy on our long voyage to the Americas!'

With her hopes raised, Mary rushed to the steps down to the beach where a group of recruits were awaiting the rowing boat from the galleon. It took her only a few moments to spot Hal from behind and run to greet him.

'Good morrow, Christopher Oak!' she called, assuming a cheerful air.

Hal turned. When he saw Mary, he took a sharp breath and made as if to ignore her.

'Cousin, 'tis no use feigning,' she cried, accosting him and dragging him from the crowd. 'I have travelled a long cold journey to bid you farewell!'

He sighed and frowned. 'Can you be sure that you were not followed?'

She raised her eyebrows. 'What do you take me for? Hal, I hear you have enlisted for America!'

Nodding, he explained his reason. 'I must put a vast ocean between me and Hugh Trevor if I am to escape the hangman, Mary. And now that you are here, you must tell my dear father that I am sorry to grieve him, and sorrier still that we will never set eyes one upon the other during this lifetime, but that hereafter, God willing, we will meet again.'

Mary promised to do this. 'Hal, I do not for one moment believe you are guilty; no more do Bess and Marion, nor any of the other servants at Saltleigh. And if by any means we can prove your innocence, we will do so.'

'Much good may it do me in the forests of America!' Hal's gloomy face stared far out to sea. 'I am voyaging with Sir Humphrey Gilbert on the "Anne Archer",' he told her. 'Pray for my soul, Mary, for there are many dangers between me and the distant shore.'

'I will pray every day,' she promised. 'You will be sorely missed.'

'By whom?' he asked. 'By my father and that is all. None else cares for a boy such as I.'

Mary took his hand between her trembling fingers. 'I care for you, Hal.'

He nodded and at last looked up. 'Mary, I have never had neither brother nor sister, but I hold you in my heart as dear as any sister, and after the death of your father I had hoped to care for you as such.'

Mary sighed. 'To know this is more to me than anything.'

'Dear cousin!' For once, Hal gave way to his feelings and let tears come to his eyes. Then he quickly brushed them away and pointed to the boat approaching the shore. 'The "Anne Archer" is a proud ship,' he said, jutting out his chin. 'She sets out to discover new territory for the Queen and return laden with treasure!'

'Then you will perhaps make your fortune as you dreamed,' she said wistfully.

'But do not look to see me these five years,' he warned.

'Hal, you will be twenty and I eighteen!' she cried, clinging on to his hand. ' 'Tis half a lifetime!'

'You will be eighteen and wed to a broad-faced fisherman, with a brood of chicks to care for.'

'Never! Hal, you must take care!'

'As must you, cousin. Tell me one thing, Mary, before I go. I know there is a weight around your heart, more even than the death of your father could cause. It drains your strength and subdues your spirit. What is it that ails you?'

'Nothing!' she said, too hastily brushing aside the question.

'I am for America, Mary, and may never return. Your secret is safe with me.'

Mary closed her eyes. The knowledge hammered at her heart to be let out into the open. 'Tell no one!' she begged.

'Upon my life!'

She inhaled then released the burden. ' 'Twas murder!' she breathed.

'Who was killed; your father, John?'

She nodded. 'I saw him stabbed to the heart.'

'By whom?' Hal's shocked eyes searched her face.

The rowing boat arrived at the shore with a crunch of pebbles. Waves lapped around Mary's ankles. 'I dare not say!'

'Give me a name and a reason!' he pleaded as impatient men called for Christopher Oak.

'I cannot!' Her promise to her father constricted her throat and stole her voice.

Hal looked into her soul. 'Hugh Trevor!' he whispered.

She did not reply. She saw a burly sailor accost Hal and take him to the boat, watched the oars dip into the water and carry him away.

Hal waved and she waved back, standing alone on the shore.

Ten

On her return to Saltleigh, Mary scarcely cared whether or not she was seen. She rode home in broad daylight, defying the protests of the grooms in the yard and the furious ranting of Lady Anne herself.

'You have been to seek out the miscreant, Hal!' she cried, calling the steward to come and punish Mary as she crept up the oak staircase with her panels of velvet. 'You make a dangerous alliance with one bound for the gallows, and I will have you beaten until you confess where he is hiding!'

From along the gallery, Kathryn and Jayne watched with smug satisfaction.

Pinned against the high wall, Mary offered no resistance.

'Take her and whip her!' the mistress of the house ordered. 'Do not spare the rod, for she is a stubborn girl with a hard spirit which must be broken.'

Trevor moved in to seize Mary, amazed by his good fortune. The sneaking, spying child had fallen deep into his trap by creeping off to see Hal; what now could be easier than to discredit her and have her thrown out of the household?

The steward's loathsome touch made Mary struggle. She bit his fingers and twisted out of his grasp, leaping down the stairs as he cursed and gave chase. He cornered her under the Campernowne coat of arms, raised his stout staff and brought it down hard on Mary's back.

'Witch!' Kathryn shrieked, stamping her feet. 'Have her burnt, Mother, for the hideous monster that she is!'

'What talk of burning?' Raleigh's voice rose above the hubbub. He came striding across the wide entrance hall, slapping his leather gauntlets against his thigh after an early morning canter with Gresham. 'Steward, who gave you leave to strike my little seamstress?'

Gasping from pain yet determined not to cry out, Mary slithered to the ground, where she lay half senseless.

' 'Tis my Lady's instruction,' Trevor said hastily and in a low voice. 'Else I would not have laid hold of her, I swear!'

'And it is my wish that you leave her to recover,' Raleigh snapped, wrenching the staff from him and looking up angrily at Lady Anne before he stooped to raise Mary.

'She meets hugger mugger with the thief!' Lady Anne rushed downstairs in a flurry of taffeta and frills. 'She is in *my* employ, Raleigh, and I will treat her as she deserves.'

With his arm around Mary's waist to support her, Raleigh's face took on an amused, cynical look. 'I merely say, mistress, that a needlewoman who is beaten black and blue, with bloodied limbs and broken fingers, is of no use to anyone. For that reason, and for no other, I wish to keep her whole!'

'Say you so!' Lady Anne snorted. 'Yet I know your tricks, Raleigh. My husband gives you free rein in this house, blind fool that he is, but I watch you closely and see your motives!'

'Then you are wiser than I believed,' came the suave reply. 'Mistress, I hardly know my *own* motives, let alone those of another. In any case, I assure you that my reasons here are purely materialistic. As I told you once already, upon this girl's skill depends the success of my appearance at Greenwich.'

'Yes, and your talk is always of your self, as if you were the brightest star in all the heavens!' Still furious but increasingly helpless, Lady Anne was reduced to a stream of insults. 'You think yourself witty and charming with your verses and your smooth flattery, but you are a vain fool, nephew, and you will come to nought!'

Raleigh gave an ironic bow. 'I thank you for your advice, Aunt, and will take care to remember it in time to come, when I may have the opportunity to advance you in fortune and in rank!'

Then, still supporting Mary, he made his way up the stairs past Kathryn and Jayne, along the gallery into the withdrawing chamber.

'Sit,' he told her, changing his brittle tone and speaking more kindly. 'It seems your ride to Plymouth was unwise.'

Mary looked startled.

'Gresham and I spied you coming through the copse by the cottage,' he explained. ' 'Twas a cold morning to be out in, Mary. Was your cousin grateful?'

She blushed but did not deny anything.

'Is he safe?'

'Yes, sir. And innocent of any wrongdoing!'

Raleigh smiled. 'I see a blow with a stick has not dampened your spirit! Now listen, child, there is a new plan afoot to remove from here to Gresham's house at Greenwich, and I wish you to make the journey with us.'

She stiffened and became wary. 'I have never been long from Saltleigh, sir. I think I should not be content.'

'And are you content here?' Raleigh crouched at her side. 'Come, child, take courage. And do not be afraid that I will abuse and mistreat you, despite what they say. My reputation is somewhat sullied, I admit, but you will find me an honourable man at heart.'

'And what will become of me at Greenwich?' she asked plainly.

'I will install you at Gresham's place, and you will sew like an angel, Mary, until my cloak is covered in work of silver and gold, encrusted with pearls and lined with sable. You have but six days to finish it and earn the glory that you deserve!'

She looked at him closely as he veered from gentle seriousness to lightheartedness, detecting what she thought was sincerity in his large, clear eyes. 'And after the cloak is made?' she asked.

'Why, the Queen comes to Greenwich!'

'And after that?' she insisted.

Raleigh laughed. 'Am I a fortune-teller, Mary? Nay, I am but a plain sailor and an indifferent poet! But seriously, when the Queen comes, a wide door opens on to a future as yet unknown. In short, we must wait and see.'

Later that night Mary had time to consider her choices. She had sewn during the day, then spoken with her uncle at supper, describing how she had seen Hal set off for a new life in the Americas under Sir Humphrey Gilbert.

'And the boy was hale?' David had asked, sadness marking his features. The tailor was a man of few words, sturdier than his dead brother, John, with a less inquiring frame of mind. All his life he had been content to serve.

'He was perfectly well, Uncle; only sorry that he had not time to bid you farewell, but convinced that his was the right course of action.'

David had shielded his eyes with his broad hand as the chatter at the dining board had grown hushed. 'I never will see him more,' he whispered.

'Fear not, David!' Jeremy had cried. 'The lad has a good head on his shoulders and as ready a pair of hands as ever was. Time will see Hal return to us a fine, fully-grown man, ready to challenge Master Trevor and his trumped-up charge!'

But a father who has lost his son cannot be so easily comforted, and David had bowed his head in sorrow, refusing to eat.

'I thank you for news of Hal, child,' he had said quietly to Mary after supper. 'Though I hear that you were beaten for your pains?'

'I expected worse,' Mary had replied, then told him of Raleigh's intervention and his wishes to take her with him to Greenwich. 'I do not want to go, Uncle, though I have little enough to keep me here at Saltleigh.'

'What we desire is scarcely to be considered,' he had advised. 'The fate of such as us is in the hands of others, and may the good Lord protect us.'

The humble words had lodged in Mary's head, and now that she lay on her mattress reflecting at the end of the day, she took issue with them. We are no mere dolls or puppets, she thought, to be played with and tossed away! Neither are we onlookers on our own lives, content to be pushed hither and thither by events. If that were so, then Hal would be this minute clapped in irons and lying in a Plymouth dungeon. No, we must think for ourselves, and if those who have authority over us behave unjustly, we must use our wits to escape that injustice! So thought Mary, alone in the world, with nothing but a fiery independence of spirit to her name.

She mocked herself then. Easier said than done! This fine talk of injustice leads nowhere, for when I rise in the morning I face the choice of staying to be hounded by Kathryn and Jayne, tormented by Lady Anne, and suspected by Trevor, or of leaving with Raleigh to God knows what future!

Or of creeping away this minute and finding my way on foot to Plymouth. For a while Mary considered this third prospect. No doubt she could wrap herself in a shawl and retread the path that Heather had taken her twenty-four hours before. She could enter the overhanging streets and be swallowed up.

'Mistress, what do you lack?' the apprentices would cry, and she would confess that she lacked money, a place to live and work to occupy her, but that she was a fine seamstress, used to fancy work of all kinds: chain stitch and coral stitch, Florentine stitch and flame stitch, laid work and couched work. The eager lads would drag her in to the dark workshops and present her to their greedy masters: fat men with gold chains and a hunger to make money, who might lock her in an attic and not feed her, but work her until her fingers were bone and then throw her on to the street for a pauper's death and funeral.

No, she was not as brave as Hal, neither was her situation so desperate.

I will go to Greenwich, she decided. Come what may.

On a clear day in early January, Mary left her home of more than thirteen years.

There were dark looks from Lady Anne and her daughters as they passed through the courtyard where Raleigh and Gresham had grooms load two packhorses with possessions they would need in town.

'Take care with that hessian parcel!' Raleigh warned. 'Guard it with your life, for 'tis the precious cloak!'

Lady Anne marched stiffly by in a gossamer-fine ruff and green velvet gown. She cast a disdainful eye at Mary's drab kersey dress with its plain criss-crossed lacing to the bodice and short grey shawl, her hair covered by a linen cap covered with a tall felt hat.

'See how she travels in the dead of winter,' Jayne sniggered, staring up at Mary already seated in the saddle; 'without busk or farthingale!'

'Why, Jayne, you may give her your old roll farthingale, shaped like a boiling sausage, for she will not know that the bum roll is quite out of fashion in town, and she may go about the streets of Greenwich in it and cause much merriment there!' Kathryn enjoyed the imagined scene before her mother chided her and swept her on into the house.

'We shall see you at Greenwich, Aunt,' Raleigh called after her. 'And my pretty cousins too!' Then he and Gresham went in search of Sir Sydney to give him sincere thanks for all that he had done for them.

Meanwhile, Mary found time to dismount and seek out her friends in the workshop. For the last time she entered the attic room with its rows of tables and benches, to the sound of snipping shears and low chatter, and the sight of many heads bowed low over the close, careful work.

'This is a fine adventure!' Bess told her cheerfully when she learned that it was time to say goodbye. 'Why, Mary, at your age I would have given my eye teeth to embark on such a thing!'

Mary sank gratefully into the older woman's ample embrace.

'Make us proud of you, child,' Marion told her. 'And tell Sophia how the cloak is accepted at court, so that she may bring news back from town.'

'And, Mary, do not let your head swell too big for your felt hat!' Bess joked, holding her now at arm's length. 'My, child, you are skin and bone. You must eat more heartily and put on flesh, else you will disappear!'

'And give Sophia all the court gossip,' Marion pressed. 'How Raleigh is received by the Queen, and which fashion is the flavour of the moment.'

'Never mind the foolish gossip.' Casting Marion to one side, Bess gave Mary one last hug. ' 'Tis you I am thinking of, child. I will not rest easy until I hear word that you are well.'

'I will take care to keep healthy,' Mary assured her.

'I hear there are creeping fogs in the city of London and foul stenches in the streets,' Bess warned. 'And I have heard of the time when bodies were piled upon bodies as the plague carts passed by!'

'Hush, Bess!' Marion intervened. 'Greenwich is not London. Anyway, 'tis winter. Mary will be well.'

'I must go,' Mary told them hastily. 'Bid me God speed.'

'With all our hearts,' Bess murmured, rapidly dissolving into tears and shaking throughout her frame.

Thus Mary turned her back on the weeping women and on all she had known.

Eleven

'The true man of fashion requires three cloaks,' Gresham was saying in his high, mocking voice as the journey to Greenwich neared its end. 'One for the morning, one for afternoon and one for evening.'

Raleigh laughed. 'Then what say you of a man who owns above ten cloaks?'

'I say he is extravagance itself!' the student laughed back. 'What need do you have of more than three?'

'Don't question the need. A man's apparel has to do with his importance at court, and well you know it. He must have a cassock and a gaberdine, as well as a mandeville worn Collie-Westonward, as they say in the north!'

'Aye, and a more senseless garment I never did see!' Gresham challenged. 'Mistress Mary, what do you say to this thing which is half-jacket, half-cloak whose side seams hang open, with one sleeve hanging down the front and the other behind?'

'Not so foolish as satin pouches which hang below the trunk hose,' she ventured, 'or stockings cross-gartered, which I have heard is the fashion at court.'

'Ha, the maid has a good eye for the ridiculousness of a gentleman's dress!' Gresham teased. After two days of hard riding together, he felt entitled to include the girl in his and Raleigh's casual conversations.

Riding ahead, Raleigh spurred his horse to the brow of a nearby hill. 'We must send Mary to the sign of the White Bear in Cheapside, to buy silks and damasks from Persia, embroidered velvet from Genoa, satins from Lucca, and all manner of fine cloths from the most renowned mercers.'

'Sir Baptist Hicks provides the best Italian fustians,' Gresham continued. 'While Sir William Stone is the place for your finest cloth of gold.'

To Mary, talk of such richness grew tedious. As if men were made of taffeta and chamblet, she thought, and not of brave deeds and refined thought. Still, Gresham had kept her amused during the long journey and the short nights of rest at the inns on the way. He had told witty tales of Oxford alehouses, where the best scholars would behave no better than country fools, and of his callow friends, in love with the idea of love, who went courting the fine young ladies of the town, who would then spurn them and send them back to college in fits of black despair.

'Ah me!' Gresham would cry, imitating a lovelorn sigh. 'Mildred has cast me aside for another, and now I must drown in a lake of tears!'

Mary smiled to herself, thinking how the scholar should learn to act wisely himself before mocking others.

Now though, as Raleigh paused to look down on the spreading city of London, at the winding river running like a silver ribbon through a grey winter's landscape, Gresham's familiarity with Mary went one step further.

'What say you to life in town, Mary-Maria, oh mistress of mine heart?'

'I hope I shall be content, sir, and fulfil my task to the best of my ability.'

'Oh come! A girl like you must dream of more than cutting and stitching,' Gresham cajoled. 'There is grandeur here beyond belief, and Greenwich is but a foothold into a life of luxury.'

'For some,' she admitted. 'But not for me.'

Gresham laughed. 'Your simplicity becomes you, child. But have you not heard of low-born girls such as you learning to please the ladies and the gentlemen at court?'

She frowned. 'Perhaps, sir, but what then?'

'Listen.' Gresham leaned closer towards her. 'Your skill with the needle pleases Walter, and it will please the ladies who attend the Queen. There will be Lady Such-and-Such, who will want to steal you from Raleigh to make her gowns, or the Duchess of So-and-So who will command you to embroider her collars. Thence you will be whisked off to become companion to a noble lady, perhaps even the highest in all the land . . .'

'Gresham, do not fill Mary's head with foolishness and vanity!' Raleigh interrupted sharply as he rode back down the hill. 'I like her as she is: plain Mary with both feet on the ground.'

And fully intent on staying that way, she thought, though she did allow herself to dream a little as they came to Greenwich. Harmless hopes of finishing Raleigh's cloak and having it admired, of saying that it was all due to her dear father, in whose memory she had made the finest garment the world had seen . . .

'Tread carefully through the mud,' Raleigh told Mary as she stepped down from the saddle outside Gresham's house overlooking the great River Thames. 'Your shoes are of open weave cloth and will spoil easily.'

Mary glanced down at her feet and at the footwear she had borrowed from Marion. The soles were of rough leather, but the uppers were flimsy. Blushing at the sight of her common shoes, she accepted her employer's help to jump the mire.

'You are as light as a feather!' Raleigh remarked, setting her down.

'Or a flea. Take care she does not bite and suck your blood!' Gresham teased, going on to make a coarse joke which Mary did not understand.

Instead, she looked up at the tall house with long windows and fancy brickwork, topped by high, thin chimneys sending out black smoke into the foggy air. The heavy oak door hung open and she glimpsed servants flanking each side of the narrow hallway, peering out at the arrivals.

At first Mary was reluctant to go through the main entrance; something which she had never been permitted to do at Saltleigh. Overcoming a revulsion to the strong, stale odours all around, she turned to look at the river teeming with sailing ships, at the baskets piled high at the quaysides and the heavy anchors stacked against a wall. It was a busy scene of men carrying, tugging, lifting and heaving, of women trudging through muddy puddles without looking up, and children apparently too cold and hungry to play. Then way across the river she noticed more rows of tall houses, some leaning, some straight, with more streets leading down to the quays and the spires of many churches rising high into the cloudy sky.

'Come inside,' Gresham urged her, flinging his travelling cloak at a manservant and striding towards a great, warm hearth. 'Margaret, you are to treat this girl well and make sure she lacks for no bodily comfort,' he instructed his housekeeper who approached with keys jangling at her waist. 'She may keep to her own bedchamber at the back of the house, where she will work for Raleigh and must not be disturbed.'

The severe-looking woman dressed in a black gown with narrow ruff and with a chignon set at the back of her head, nodded slightly and told Mary to follow her.

'Three days, Mary!' Raleigh reminded her before she mounted the shiny oak stairs. 'The Queen comes to Greenwich this Friday. Shall you finish on time?'

'I will not sleep until I do,' she promised, aware of all eyes upon her mud-spattered skirt and red, frost-pinched hands and face.

'You are in a new town amongst strangers,' he said. 'But do not be cast down. You heard Gresham; you will be well cared for.'

'I am not cast down,' she replied, as steadily as she could.

But when she got to her room and saw that the window faced on to another wall across a small yard, and that the four-poster bed filled most of the cramped space, she felt her lip begin to quiver. And when the housekeeper cast her a look of piercing disdain she let her head drop and shoulders sag.

'Why is the great Walter Raleigh showing special favour to a little country slattern such as you?' Margaret asked unabashed. 'You dress coarsely, child, and bring the smells of the stable along with you.'

'That I do not!' Mary argued proudly. 'And better any day the smells of the country than the stench of the town!'

Margaret shrugged, then went to smooth and pat the embroidered counterpane. 'You never slept on a feather mattress, did you child?'

'I never lacked sleep for the want of a soft bed, you may be sure.'

The housekeeper turned at the spirited reply. She stared but said nothing more, sweeping her keys up into her hand and swinging them as she went out.

Then Mary sat in the narrow window seat, looking miserably out of the window. With a pang she thought of the elm trees behind Saltleigh Hall and the hills that rolled down to the sea. At least I have the river and the sound of the water lapping against the quay, she thought, clinging to any natural sound. But I shall miss the flutter of leaves on the trees and the soft rustle of grasses. Why, here I can scarcely see the clouds in the sky for the sloping red roofs and tall smoking chimneys!

Soon, however, the parcel containing Raleigh's cloak was carried up to her and she set herself to work. If she could no longer see the birds in the branches, then she would work them into the velvet; so like life that it seemed the robin's breast at the hem of each panel would swell and he would sing his sweet song. To Mary, the clusters of seed pearls which she sewed to the worked holly branches became the red berries of the tree itself, and she could smell the sap, hear the crackle and spit of the leaves as they were piled on to a bonfire whenever autumn came.

Her fingers flew across the cloth, weaving her precious memories into Raleigh's cloak. And, for a while, she was content.

Wednesday came, and with it news of the Queen.

'They say Leicester has spoken for you,' Gresham told Raleigh. 'He has told the Queen that you will attend here at Greenwich, and she has not flown into a fury, nor threatened you with the executioner's axe!'

'I owe Leicester my most devout thanks,' Raleigh remarked, pacing the area in front of the hearth in the hallway.

'They say too that Elizabeth is troubled abroad by the Spanish and at home by the Pope,' his friend added, speaking openly in front of Mary, who had been called to exhibit the progress of her work. 'The Catholics cause her to lose sleep by stirring from their secret corners of this far-flung kingdom. She has sworn to root them out of their priestholes and send them hurtling into Hell!'

Mary's hand came to rest on the soft pile of the sable fur with which she was lining the cloak. She glanced up at Raleigh with troubled eyes.

'Did you know that the Earl of Oxford is suspected of links with Rome?' Gresham whispered. 'And that all who claim him as a friend may be tainted?'

'Say you not so!' Raleigh stopped and hung his head. 'For God's sake, man, who is there in this land who does not have some distant cousin or acquaintance who tastes wine from the Catholic chalice? In any case, Oxford and I quarrelled before I was flung in Marshalsea, so there is no danger to me there!'

But danger lurks elsewhere! Mary thought, quivering at the memory of hushed whispers and shadows in the workroom, of strangers who brought news from Rome and wielded the knife against her father, and of Trevor's treacherous plot.

Speak out! she told herself. Now, this instant, while there is talk of priestholes and Hell! But her hands trembled and her heart wasn't strong enough. They will not believe me, she thought. Gresham will laugh, and Raleigh will say I have foolish nightmares. Besides; there is my promise!

So the moment passed, and the men's earnest talk was succeeded by the usual boasts and banter.

'Mary mine!' Gresham sang out, bending his knee and holding up his leg. 'What say you to the curve of my calf? Will it cut a dash during the jig and the courante? Or should I pad it out with bombast 'neath my silken stockings?'

'I should not risk bombast close to their lordships' rapiers,' she answered gamely. 'For the sharp points will rip the silk and the stuffing will run out!'

Raleigh laughed. 'You must have a new gown, child, and come to court with us. Margaret shall send to the tailor for one of tawny silk, which will suit your colouring, and you shall sit in the gallery and watch Gresham dance the gavotte!'

Mary's face flushed deep red. 'Indeed, sir,' she muttered uncertainly.

'Yes indeed!' The notion appealed to Raleigh and he pressed on with it, calling the housekeeper and ordering 'a gown of tawny chamblet, which is silk and camel hair mixed and is better to keep warm in during this wintry weather. It shall be adorned with ruff and ribbons, and of the latest fashion!'

'Of what size shall this gown be?' thin-lipped Margaret demanded. 'And for whom shall I buy it?'

'For Mary Devereux, mistress!' Raleigh exclaimed. 'Our little seamstress is to come to court!'

'Raleigh, did you know that there was a Devereux at the court of the Queen's father?' Gresham remarked after the disgruntled housekeeper had gone about her errand.

The men had kept Mary with them as she put the finishing touches to the cloak.

Raleigh looked up from the letter he was writing at a table by the window. 'Tell us more, Gresham, and let us speculate on these Devereux!'

'Sir Roland Devereux was a Frenchman and Master of Queen Anne Boleyn's Wardrobe, married to Isabella. They were never blessed with issue, and indeed Sir Roland fell suddenly out of favour when Queen Anne so unfortunately lost her head. The Devereux fled back to Paris, but 'twas rumoured that Sir Roland had fathered a bastard child who remained behind.'

'How do you come to know this?' Raleigh challenged, still allowing himself to be distracted from his letter.

'My father often hunted with Henry's courtiers,' Gresham explained. 'I had forgot the name of Devereux until you called Mary by her family name. But then I recalled the stories of drinking and wenching after the hunt.'

'Ah, so now we have Sir Roland fathering a child; a son who was sent out of the way to the country, and who remained behind when the father fled!' Raleigh spun the story further still. 'Now, Mary, are you listening? Devereux is an uncommon name in England, is it not? Suppose that your father the tailor was the very son to whom Gresham alludes? Would that not be a thing indeed?'

At this Mary stood up and made to leave the room. 'My father is dead, sir, and cannot answer the accusation!'

'Stop, child!' Barring her way yet realising that he had offended her, Raleigh became grave. 'This is no accusation but a passport into a life beyond your wildest dreams! Where is the shame in your father being born a bastard, Mary? Come, 'tis only country folk who take offence from such matters.'

Almost in tears, Mary argued on. 'Well then, sir, my father has a brother, David, yet living at Saltleigh. How does that suit your suspicions about his begetting?'

'Two illegitimate sons to the same mother!' Gresham cut in admiringly. 'Why, Sir Roland was a sportsman indeed!'

'Let me pass!' Mary demanded, thrusting the cloak at Raleigh. 'I will not stay to be made the butt of your cruel jokes, nor to hear my father's name dragged into the mire.'

Raleigh sighed. 'You do not understand. I am finding you a foothold into the world of the Queen's court! What would you do: live like the poor girls and women you see here on the streets?'

'Yes, if it is honourable.' Moved beyond endurance, Mary tried to push her way up the stairs, but a hammering at the door broke into the argument.

It was opened to Hugh Trevor, with news from Saltleigh.

'I felt sure to find you here,' the steward explained breathlessly, as if he had run all the way from Devon. 'I arrived with Lady Anne not two hours since. She stays at lodgings across the river with her maid, Sophia.'

Mary had rarely seen Trevor out of breath and in disarray. Yet here he stood, blown by the wind and spattered by mud thrown up from carts on the busy streets.

Raleigh offered a cold welcome. 'What is it to me that my aunt has found unfashionable lodgings? She can sleep with the horses in their stables for all I care.'

Trevor ventured a sycophantic smile. 'It pleases you to jest, yet her Ladyship bade me seek you out to say that she has come without her daughters, Kathryn and Jayne, for they have fallen sick to an illness as yet unknown and are too ill to travel.'

'Then she has broken their hearts,' Raleigh scoffed. 'Those girls put their lifeblood into appearing before the

Queen and finding themselves husbands! What will happen now to their farthingales and frills?'

Listening from the foot of the stairs, Mary felt a mean-spirited surge of satisfaction. So Jayne and Kathryn were not to display their jackanapes jigs at court after all! And she, Mary Devereux, would be the one to witness the untold splendour instead.

'Lady Anne was eager still to come as ambassador for the Campernowne family,' Trevor went on. 'She craves a favour from you, sir, in the name of her husband and the generosity he has displayed towards you of late.'

Raleigh grunted ungraciously. 'Name the favour,' he muttered.

' 'Tis the support of your arm to escort her to court. In short, will you escort her before the Queen tomorrow?'

'I had rather swallow hot coals!' Raleigh fumed.

Gresham laughed out loud. 'Why, Raleigh, you are twenty-eight years old, not so very much below your aunt's age, which we would put at, say, thirty-five, give or take a decade or two!'

'Thirty-eight at least,' his friend shot back.

'What is so very unnatural about the match?' Gresham insisted. 'The Queen herself is forty-eight, and yet you fancy yourself a suitable suitor!'

'And most like to make a commendable couple,' Trevor said soothingly. 'What is age where true beauty and majesty shine through?'

'This fellow's tongue is smooth as silk!' Gresham laughed.

'Go tell your mistress that I will be no escort to an unrelenting shrew and harpie, let her paint an inch thick,' Raleigh decided. 'Even upon my uncle's life, I would not wear such a clog around my neck and thus miss my chance with the Queen!'

'That's it, straight and strong, Walter!'

Mary hardly heard the student's crowing comment for studying Trevor. The steward's eyes darted here and there, though his mouth wore a fixed smile. She saw that his restless, devious mind was working out the next move.

'Shall I tell her this, or make some excuse?' Trevor inquired civilly, finally catching his breath and assuming his usual smooth control.

'Word for word!' Raleigh insisted.

'Then shall I fall out of favour, for the bearer of bad news is never thanked.'

'Yes, Raleigh, you will get this fine fellow dismissed from his post!' Gresham guffawed, while Mary watched in cold silence.

Raleigh paused for thought, but the notion of humiliating his aunt even at second hand was too strong to resist. 'Tell her that I say she is but a poor excuse for a lady of high estate,' he insisted. 'And when you have done, return here to this house, for Gresham lacks a clever steward to look after his affairs, do you not, Gresham?'

All at once Mary's cold hostility turned to burning fear. It seemed that Raleigh was intent on drawing the venomous enemy into his very bosom.

'Do I?' His unwary friend was slow to catch Raleigh's drift.

'Yes, you do. And here is the very man,' Raleigh insisted, drawing them together and slapping them both on the back. 'Gresham, here is Hugh Trevor. Hugh Trevor, here is Gresham; from henceforth master and man!'

Twelve

The cloak was finished.

Mary sat back late on Thursday night, her hands aching with the constant pulling of thread and tying of knots. She sighed and eased her back by pressing with both thumbs against the base of her spine.

It was finished.

She went and spread Raleigh's cloak on her silk counterpane, passing her fingers over the raised patterns and gems. The deep pile of the black velvet was soft to the touch. It glowed sumptuously in the candlelight.

Another sigh and a small smile showed that Mary was pleased with her work. How she had cherished these patterns as she created them, and how proud she would be when Raleigh wore it to meet the Queen.

Later, as Mary undressed for bed, a message came via Margaret the housekeeper that Raleigh wanted to see her in the great hall. 'He wishes to see his cloak,' Margaret reported.

' 'Tis on the bed. You may take it to him,' Mary replied wearily, standing in her plain shift, with bare feet.

'I am ordered to bring the little seamstress too,' Margaret said with a raised eyebrow. 'It seems one will not do without the other.'

So Mary put on her plain grey gown and went downstairs, to find Raleigh and Gresham flushed with wine, together with the stiff, silent figure of Hugh Trevor standing to one side of the hearth. She held up the cloak as commanded, letting its folds hang softly and showing the glint of the pearls in the firelight.

' 'Tis perfect, is it not, Gresham?' Raleigh proclaimed. 'Did you ever see such curious work?'

' 'Twill beat all other cloaks at the court for originality and faultless technique,' Gresham assured him.

'Elizabeth will notice it. She is accomplished in fine needlework herself, and will ask to know how it was done. I will stand tall and wear it draped across one shoulder, Spanish style. I will tell her of my little Devereux seamstress and say that Mary shall work her a gift of cutwork cuffs flourished with silver and silks of many colours!'

'The New Year is a time for such gifts,' his friend encouraged, but he evidently grew weary of the topic which so fascinated Raleigh and began instead to flirt with Mary. 'Mistress, come here and sit upon my knee while I teach you court manners,' he suggested. 'If you wish to improve yourself you must pay heed!'

'I have no wish to improve myself,' Mary retorted. 'Nor to sit on your knee, sir.'

Raleigh laughed and turned to Trevor. 'Would you say that the girl lacks cunning for her advancement, steward? I ask you in particular because I judge you to have certain skill in that direction!'

Mary saw Trevor's eyes flicker then open wide. 'I would estimate that Mistress Mary has more guile than you might suppose,' he replied. 'Do not be fooled by simple appearances in women, for they often conceal secretive natures.'

'Hah, 'tis true!' Raleigh took the cloak from Mary and swung it around his shoulders. Then he strutted across the hall. 'See how it hangs and catches the light. Mary, did you hear that your former mistress at Saltleigh, my esteemed aunt, has dismissed her steward as we foretold, and falls back upon the generosity of her old friend, Lady Grace Holby, with whom she will be presented at court tomorrow?'

'Her *very* old friend!' Gresham emphasised. 'And a widow who has buried four husbands, each one richer than the last!'

'I am glad of it,' Mary said quietly, anxious to leave. She escaped Gresham's outstretched arms and backed towards the staircase.

'Not so glad as I am to have the witch out of my hair!' Raleigh exclaimed, swirling the cloak as he turned. 'Mary, do not be so eager to retire, but stay a little and enjoy your work.'

'I am weary, sir.'

'What, and not excited by the prospect of tomorrow? Child, you must know that every soul in this nation would long to see the Queen, but only a few achieve their dream. 'Tis very heaven to be included in her court, for she is the Sun, the Moon and all the planets in the night sky. She is incomparably above and beyond us all!'

At Raleigh's glowing enthusiasm Mary did indeed feel a stirring of expectation. 'Will she come by boat?' she asked.

'By royal barge, like her father King Henry, to her house here in Greenwich. There will be boats fore and aft, filled with courtiers, resplendent with banners. She will step out on to the quay to the blare of golden trumpets. Men will cheer her and women will lean from the windows to wave their kerchiefs.'

'Stop!' Gresham begged. 'Or even *I* shall not sleep for expectation of the event.'

At last Raleigh relented. 'Go to your beds then, sleep and dream of the morrow. Rise early and dress in your finery, for the Queen comes at noon and we must make ready!'

Next day Margaret came to Mary's chamber at dawn. She placed a candle at the bedside and shook her awake, telling her to stir herself while she brought the new tawny gown from the servants' quarters.

Sleepily, Mary turned her head towards the stern housekeeper. 'I am sorry to have you woken so soon,' she apologised. ' 'Tis scarcely light.'

'I do as I am bid,' the woman said abruptly, disappearing for a while then returning with clothes in rich gold, worked with swirling designs of red and green. ' 'Twas the best my master's money could buy,' Margaret told Mary cuttingly, 'though nothing in comparison with the gowns embroidered by ladies at court.'

Shivering in the morning cold, Mary stepped quickly into a pure white smock made of finest linen. Margaret stood by with a whalebone stiffened bodice which went over the smock and came low at the front, laced at each side and made tight as could be.

'Here is the petticoat,' the housekeeper said. 'Take care how you step into it, for the farthingale is already tied in place.'

Once more Mary obeyed, surprised at the weight of the padding which broadened the skirt, and how the corset and petticoat hampered her movement. 'I'm glad I must not wear this for every day!' she sighed. ' 'Tis too much work!'

In spite of her generally disapproving air, the middle-aged woman smiled. 'They say that there is no beauty without pain,' she remarked, offering Mary stockings of white silk and shoes of red Spanish leather.

'Did *you* ever go to court?' Mary inquired, catching a

glimpse of herself in a looking-glass which hung by the bed. Her waist seemed more slender than ever, her skin pale against the richness of the tawny silk.

'Once, when I was a child and my mother was nursemaid to the Queen's half-sister, Princess Mary. I remember little, except that the ladies' hands were thin and beautiful and they carried fans to drive away the foul air.'

Mary grew more curious about her dresser. 'And have you married?' she asked.

'Aye, and borne two sons, both now at sea,' Margaret admitted. 'I have lost a seafaring husband to a storm off the coast of western France, but still the boys would follow their father. I pray for their souls each morning and night, that they may be safely returned to me.'

Mary thought then of Hal, and how he must face the ocean's roar. 'Are there many dangers at sea?' she asked, fearing an honest reply.

'Every hour of every day,' the woman confirmed. 'Water is a mighty force when angered. No ship can help being driven on to rocks in a gale, or being smashed to pieces by the waves.'

'But there may not be storms. What if the sea remains calm?'

'Then there is fever in the ports and starvation at sea. Many die.'

So her cousin had small hope of escaping the risks.

Mary sighed as she stepped into her fine shoes, silently cursing Trevor for driving Hal from Saltleigh.

'We must dress your hair,' Margaret informed her, shaking herself free of fearful thoughts for her sons. 'Come, child, make haste and sit by the window.'

Forcing herself to keep still while the housekeeper drew back her long curls and pinned them in a high chignon, Mary studied her image in the glass. She scarcely recognised what she saw. The face in the mirror was a perfect oval, the eyes large and rich chestnut brown, the lashes dark and casting shadows over her cheek. Every trace of a curl in her hair had vanished; instead it was straightened and raised, fastened in place on the crown by a heart-shaped decoration of gold and pearls. Her long white neck was bare until Margaret placed a cutwork rebato around the square opening of her bodice, wiring it in place so that it stood up at the back and fell gracefully on to her breast.

'There!' The housekeeper stood back to survey her work.

'Am I made ready?' Mary asked.

'But for this necklace of simple pearls.' With one last detail and deft movements of her fingers Margaret completed the picture. 'Now you may stand in the gallery at the Queen's house and you will not disgrace any master in this land!'

Elizabeth Tudor's house at Greenwich stood not three hundred paces from the front door to Gresham's place.

Raleigh gathered together Mary in her dress of gold, Trevor in his sober black suit with its slashed sleeves and modest ruff, and Gresham, resplendent in scarlet peascod doublet with small trunk hose and many strings of pearls worn like a sash across his chest.

Raleigh himself had chosen a cream silk doublet artfully slashed and fastened with a row of large pearl buttons. His hose were black and decorated with more pearls, while Mary's cloak hung from one shoulder to display the silver motifs taken from nature and the Latin motto '*amor et virtute*' prominently on view. 'Black and white are the colours of the Queen,' he explained nervously to the assembled company of servants who stood in the hall ready to see them leave. 'And this silver crescent worn in my ear refers to Elizabeth as Cynthia, goddess of the moon.'

Gresham's servants nodded their approval.

'Raleigh, calm yourself, for the Queen never had a more handsome suitor!' Gresham assured him.

'Come then.' Impatiently Raleigh herded Mary and Trevor towards the door. 'Steward, we rely upon you to observe the company and report who finds favour with Leicester, for he is a man of influence and cannot be overlooked.'

Trevor bowed low and promised to fulfil this task. 'I will be your eyes and ears, sir. No passing remark or meaningful glance will go unnoticed.'

'And Mary, stand on the balcony where the Queen may see you, for I hope to point you out as the envy of all seamstresses, at here and abroad.'

Mary felt the drumbeat of her heart proclaim her own nervousness. Her mouth was dry and her small palms moist as they stepped out on to the quayside.

Straight away they were swallowed up by an immense crowd which flowed slowly towards the Queen's house. People of all quality had joined the throng, from those fine gentlemen like Raleigh and Gresham, through merchants displaying solid respectability in their plain furred cloaks and cutwork ruffs, scholars in long black gowns and soft, folded caps, to tradesmen in leather aprons and brimmed hats. Even beggars had crept in amongst the respectable people: barefoot boys leading blind men, and those who limped along on one leg with crutches under their arms.

'Make way!' Trevor ordered these commoners in a voice so stern that the crowd parted and Raleigh, head and shoulders above most in the crowd, sailed through with Mary and Gresham in tow.

Mary found that they reached the Queen's quay in time to secure a place at the front of the throng, up against a short landing stage accessed by wooden steps. She saw Raleigh bow to gentlemen of his acquaintance, many of whom eyed him coldly and asked among themselves how it was that Walter Raleigh had found the nerve to present himself in front of the Queen.

'Was he not thrown into prison for brawling?' one muttered behind his gloved hand.

'Aye, and other things beside. The fellow is lucky not to have his head displayed on a pole at Traitors' Gate!' another replied.

'Such a fall from grace calls for a grand gesture of loyalty to restore his standing in the Queen's favour,' the first opined. 'Perhaps seeking out of new territory for England's glory would do it.'

'Raleigh has not the stomach for another long voyage,' the second pointed out, well within Mary's hearing. 'Did you not hear? Gilbert has set sail for the Americas without him.'

'May the Lord preserve him and all who sail with him,' the first speaker concluded.

'See where the Queen's barge sails towards us!' a woman's voice cried from one of the windows of the houses lining the wharf.

Then everyone craned their necks and stood on tiptoe for a view of the flotilla of small boats surging under great London Bridge with its stone arches, topped by houses of four, and sometimes five, storeys, their chimneys smoking on this cold, clear day.

At first Mary could only see an array of boats without picking out the Queen's barge. It wasn't until they drew close that she made out a larger one in the centre of the formation which was topped with a white canopy adorned at each corner with silver fleurs de lys. Under the canopy sat a regal figure in a pure white dress with flaming red hair.

' 'Tis the Queen!' people whispered in awestruck voices. There was a general hush, as of held breath, and the sound of the waves lapping the wharf could clearly be heard.

The flotilla drew alongside the Queen's house before it turned in the water and headed towards the quay where Raleigh and his company stood. Trumpets were sounded by musicians in coats of orange and gold.

An awed sigh went up among the crowd: 'The Queen!'

More trumpets, then the first two boats drew up alongside the quay. Two ladies stepped out; one was dressed in white and silver, one in black and gold. Their wide skirts brushed the steps as they climbed on to the quay.

'Giovanna Tornabuoni from Venice and Magdalena, Duchess of Nuremburg,' Raleigh told Mary and Gresham. 'The Queen keeps them constantly at her side.'

Mary marvelled at the work of the ladies' ruffs and at their white hands resplendent with jewels.

'And now Elizabeth herself,' Raleigh breathed, holding himself tall and proud.

The trumpets blared once more as the Queen stepped from her barge.

Mary saw before her a small, slender woman with a very pale, almost white face. Her eyes were dark, her nose fairly long and straight, her mouth small and refined.

She moved slowly, conscious of the eyes of the adoring crowd, but looking neither to right nor left. Every detail about her appearance spoke of wealth and luxury, from the finest cutwork of her round ruff, to the pearls set into her bright red hair, to the rubies set in the centre of the satin bows attaching her wide sleeves to her long, pointed bodice and the swirling gold pattern embroidered into it.

Mary took all this in, noting the tiny white and gold slippers as the Queen ascended the steps and the fantastic designs of her skirt: purple pansies, also known as love-in-idleness, the eglantine rose, the white swan and the golden pomegranate. She was breathless with wonder, struck dumb by the beauty and luxury she beheld.

But Raleigh was in no such state of awe. He alone of the gentlemen at the quayside stepped forward as the Queen stood on the jetty. He said nothing, but used his height and stature to stand out from the crowd. His head was high, his dark beard immaculately barbered, his dark eyes looking boldly at Elizabeth.

She noticed him straight away. Her fine, arched eyebrows rose a fraction. She paused, then extended her slender hand. 'Raleigh!'

He moved towards her, Mary's cloak swinging handsomely, the lower half of his face framed by the sable collar, the intricate pattern of pearls glowing in the daylight. Then he was down on one knee, bowing his head as a loyal servant must do, waiting for a gesture from the Queen that would allow him to stand and escort her on to the quay.

'A hit!' Gresham whispered. 'Most definitely the rapier has found its target!'

Then, with a gesture of infinite grace and elegance, Elizabeth turned the palm of her hand upwards and Raleigh stood and took the hand to lead her forward.

Dizzy with the grandness of the occasion, Mary watched every gesture, every movement.

'You have been from Our court too long,' Elizabeth said to Raleigh, inclining her head, though not smiling.

'It pleases your Majesty to say so,' Raleigh replied, all deference and humility.

'We have missed you.'

This time he said nothing, but pride reappeared in his eyes and a faint smile appeared.

'We were much displeased by your excesses,' the Queen reminded him.

The smile vanished. 'I was to blame,' he admitted.

Elizabeth paused to glance back at the river. It flowed sluggish and grey under a heavy sky. 'We have a cold, dark winter ahead of Us,' she remarked. 'We need new diversions, fresh wits to amuse Us.'

Another dutiful silence from Raleigh.

'How do your pretty love sonnets and your rapier ripostes, Master Raleigh?'

'Alas; blunted by the absence of your Majesty; the only subject worthy of it,' he replied.

And now the Queen smiled. The crowd murmured and the ladies Giovanna and Magdalena gave approving taps of their fingers against their palms.

'A second hit!' Gresham breathed.

'Come!' the Queen said, asking Raleigh to lead her onwards while her retinue disembarked behind her.

She leaned on his arm and came up the steps on to the quay in stately procession, with the crowd pressing forward. Mary felt herself thrust almost to within touching distance of Raleigh.

Then the couple at the centre of attention, as the sun is in the sky, paused. Elizabeth surveyed her subjects, then glanced ahead at the way they must pass through the thronging people to the entrance to her house. It was perhaps twelve small steps across a trampled, muddy courtyard, and her way was barred by a wide puddle. She frowned and looked to her companion.

Seeing the difficulty, he acted immediately.

Mary felt the soft velvet of his cloak brush her face as he swung it from his shoulders. It glinted. The silver and gold motifs swirled by her eyes.

Then Raleigh dropped the cloak on to the ground. The Queen smiled and stepped on to it.

In a moment Mary saw her life's work and dreams trampled into the mud. 'Father!' she whispered. But no one heard, and the gentlemen and ladies of the court daintily followed the Queen and Raleigh into her house.

Thirteen

A moment, a gesture; and a dream had ended. A monarch's whim had been obeyed and Mary felt that her heart had been crushed between two great stones.

She had sat for countless hours, head bent, fingers flying over the cloth to create a perfection of cutting and stitching. It was a fine thing this cloak; lovely to the touch, dazzling to the eye. And it had contained the nature that she observed around her at Saltleigh: the birds and the trees, the soft snowflakes and the drooping, shy flowers of the hedgerows – all the gentleness of this world.

And now it was nothing. Just as Mary's father, John, was nothing. He was dead and she was alone, with no one left who mattered or whom she could hold dear.

She cried silent tears as she entered one of the grandest houses of all the land and took her place next to the minstrels in the high gallery.

'How much would you give now for the little seamstress's skill?' Hugh Trevor jeered. He had evidently watched the event with some amusement.

The jibe made Mary lift her head and stare him in the eye. Behind her the musicians tuned their stringed instruments, ready to play for the Queen. Next to her, ladies-in-waiting and other attendants looked eagerly about them.

'It seems it is not worth a farthing!' the steward said. 'Such is life when it rests on the fickle wings of fortune. One moment you are Raleigh's favourite and Gresham's plaything. The next you are forgotten!'

Mary choked back her tears and bound her sorrow into a tight knot resting against her breastbone. She vowed she would hold it there and never let it be seen. Meanwhile, Trevor moved away, busy about some important errand.

Down below in the main hall of the great house, the gentlemen of Elizabeth's court stood at ease beneath shields bearing the Queen's crest and the stuffed heads of mighty-antlered deer. The ladies arranged themselves by rank and sat under the oak-panelled gallery, ostrich feather fans wafting gently to and fro.

'My lady Duchess sits with Lady Burghley,' a nearby waiting woman pointed out to her neighbour. ' 'Tis a wonder for the two have not spoken since their falling out over an ell of cambric this spring gone by!'

'Pray do not distract me; I am admiring the Earl of Dorset's shapely calves in those scarlet silk stockings!' the other replied, making both women giggle.

Then the music began and the young men sought out

partners amongst the seated gentlewomen, some choosing the most important in rank, others making their way on to the floor with the youngest and prettiest. Looking for Raleigh, Mary saw that he had positioned himself behind the Queen's chair.

'The Queen does not dance,' one of the ladies-in-waiting remarked from the gallery.

'She is too much engaged with her new favourite,' another said.

'Or rather, old favourite made new by Leicester's recommendation.'

Soon all the talk was of Raleigh's presence at Elizabeth's side.

'They say he has put behind the excesses of his youth,' one said.

'I will not believe it until he casts off Gresham and his like.'

'Aye, and Oxford, for he is a secret Catholic,' an older, sterner servant insisted, to a chorus of alarmed whispers. 'He is indeed!' she insisted. 'There is a secret knot of them about this court, all conspiring for the Queen's overthrow, and those who deny it are blind fools!'

'Lucky for you that the musicians drown out your suspicions,' another woman told her. 'For she who dares speak such heresy before the Queen would not long keep her head!'

''Tis no heresy to speak in the Queen's defence,' the

woman asserted. 'Rather the heretics are the guilty ones that plot against her!'

Listening, Mary let the scene below her fall out of focus and remembered the furtive conversations she had seen in the corridors and workshops of Saltleigh. Until now they had grown ever more indistinct in her mind, so that she sometimes thought she had imagined Hugh Trevor meeting with strangers behind heavy curtains and in dark corners, and that their talk of the Pope had been but a dream. Even that moment when a hand had lifted the knife against her father had seemed the stuff of nightmare, except that John Devereux lay for certain in the cold ground, underneath a fresh headstone bearing his name.

Then Trevor himself rushed back along the gallery bearing a scroll sealed with ribbon and red wax. He stopped momentarily at Mary's side to pour more poisoned words into her ear. 'Who will guard you now, little seamstress?' he sneered. 'Remember that I would have your cousin Hal hung by the neck if I could but lay hands on him, and know too that my opinion of you runs no higher!'

Mary bit her lip hard and tasted blood on her tongue.

'You and he both!' Trevor insisted. 'Methinks you confided in your cousin, mistress, and that you carry a certain forbidden knowledge inside that pretty dark head!'

She stared in his eyes without blinking. It was the first time that the steward had openly declared his suspicions.

Trevor smiled. 'The proud look tells me so!' he declared.

'Beware, Mary Devereux, and say nothing of this matter, for you will not be believed!'

Over his shoulder, the players changed the tune from lively French jig to stately Spanish pavane, and the Queen and Raleigh rose to join the dance. Meanwhile, Lady Anne Campernowne's attendant, Sophia, pushed along the gallery to speak with Trevor.

'They say you bear news from Saltleigh,' Sophia began hurriedly.

'The messenger had not been told of my change of service from Campernowne to Gresham,' the steward confirmed. 'He came sweating and stinking to London by horseback and delivered this letter into my hands.'

Sophia took it from him. 'What does it say?' she demanded.

Trevor shrugged. 'The seal is unbroken. How should I know the contents?'

'Don't beat about the bush, but tell me the news as the messenger told it to you,' the Italian maid insisted.

' 'Tis nothing to me now, so here you are. The news is that a sudden fever has carried off the elder of the two daughters and that Jayne too waits at death's door. Sir Sydney would that his wife were at home to bid the younger girl farewell.'

Trevor's news, delivered without emotion, hit Mary hard. Kathryn was dead; the carping, envious girl who had tormented her had been carried from their midst almost overnight. How frail was the thread of life and how powerless all the trappings of wealth which could not protect a single soul from the wide sweep of cruel Death's scythe!

With a gasp, Sophia clutched the letter and hurried off to find her mistress. Mary watched from the gallery as the maid sought out Lady Anne amongst the ladies who sat out of the dance. She heard the slow rise and fall of the music, saw the intertwined arms of the dancers and the loving look which Raleigh bestowed on his Queen. But it was like a dumb show or an unreal masque where characters paraded made-up emotions which behind the paint and the mask were mere hollow pretence. The only solid thing is death, Mary thought, heavily.

She saw Sophia approach Lady Anne with the scroll, the latter waving dismissively until the maid insisted that she break the seal, the lady ungraciously giving way and having Sophia open the letter and read it aloud.

Mary watched Lady Anne's pale face as her one-time mistress rose to her feet clutching the low neck of her gown. Her expression hovered for a moment on the brink of untold horror then collapsed, her mouth falling open, her eyes staring in agony. The gentlewoman beside her, probably Lady Grace Holby, touched her friend's arm, only to have her recoil and run from the hall. Sophia whispered to Lady Grace, then the two women followed Lady Anne.

'And so the scene is played out,' Trevor commented. 'The grieving mother will return to Devon full of remorse. She will believe, falsely, that she could have saved her daughters' lives had she remained at Saltleigh. Guilt will lead her to repent her folly and to lead a life of utter devotion. Henceforth Sir Sydney Campernowne will never feel the sharp end of his wife's tongue for she will spend the rest of her days in humble prayer. See, 'tis a happy ending, Mistress Mary, so I advise you to waste no tears!'

Shaking her head, Mary retreated from the front of the gallery to the dark, narrow stairs leading to a long, ground-floor gallery behind the crowded hall. There she stopped to gather her thoughts, taking refuge in a deep recess overlooking the grey River Thames.

What was she to do now, she wondered. Might she return to Saltleigh now that Raleigh was finished with her and Hugh Trevor was no longer steward to Sir Sydney? Her heart longed to see it again, and yet Lady Anne would not welcome her. But then perhaps Trevor was right in foreseeing a great change in her former mistress now that Death had left his mark.

When a door opened at the far end of the gallery, Mary shrank further into the recess to avoid notice, but then realised that the couple who had retreated from the music and the gaiety were none other than Raleigh and the Queen herself.

'Here is a quiet moment to catch Our breath,' the Queen said with a sigh. 'But only a moment, We fear, before Leicester seeks us out.'

'Surely the Earl is not so jealous of his Queen that he cannot allow us a minute to ourselves!' Raleigh jested, leading Elizabeth by the hand towards the spot where Mary sat.

'Ah, jealousy!' This time the Queen's sigh was loud and sincere. ' 'Tis a thing which We must guard against, for it turns men into monsters and honest souls into deceivers.'

'Your Majesty bestows on me a great honour,' Raleigh said in a low voice.

'How so?'

'You take me into your confidence, and I a mere soldier and adventurer bent on garnering great riches for Your Majesty's coffers.' With a bow Raleigh showed his gratitude.

The Queen laughed. 'Come, I like your pride, Walter; not this shallow show of humility.'

'Walter?' he echoed.

She gave an intimate, knowing smile. 'Yes, for 'tis your name, is it not?'

He smiled back, then dropped low on to his knee. 'And 'tis yours, Majesty, and everything I have, down to the last drop of my blood!'

The Queen looked down at him more thoughtfully. 'In my heart, though my head may caution me otherwise, I do believe this to be true.'

She bade him stand and take her back into the hall, but just then the dry rustle of Mary's tawny silk skirt caught her attention. 'Stand forth!' the imperious Queen cried.

Trembling, Mary did as she was bid, head down and curtseying low.

'Why, Mary!' Raleigh exclaimed, breaking the tension of the Queen's sharp command. 'Come here, child, and do not be afraid.'

She went and stood before them, her lashes still wet with tears, her chest heaving with fright.

'Your Majesty, here is a girl of rare talent,' Raleigh insisted, in high spirits now that he had found such firm favour with the Queen. 'At her fingertips the needle flies through velvet and cloth of gold, weaving such patterns as Her Majesty herself would not believe possible! She transforms nature into artifice the like of which you have never seen.'

'She is but a child,' the Queen murmured.

'Who must make her way in the world now that her father follows her mother to the grave.'

Elizabeth softened her stance and insisted on raising Mary with her own hand. 'Who was her father?'

'John Devereux, bastard son of Sir Roland Devereux, Master of the Wardrobe to Queen Anne Boleyn,' Raleigh answered smoothly.

Mary froze and looked at the Queen with troubled eyes.

The Queen tilted her head to one side. 'Do not be afraid; the sins of the fathers shall not be visited on their children and their children's children,' she assured Mary. 'Is it true that you are an accomplished needlewoman?'

'Answer, Mary!' Raleigh encouraged, but then ran on with his praises. 'This is the little seamstress who made the cloak of pearls,' he explained.

'The cloak, Walter?' The Queen looked again at her gallant courtier then raised her eyebrows and smiled. 'Ah yes, the cloak !'

Then she turned on her heel and briskly bade him escort her back into the hall.

Fourteen

It was not until long after the Queen had left that Mary came to her senses. Stunned by the occasion, she sat back in the stone recess trying to gather herself together and decide on the course she should take next.

Here am I, a girl from the country without employment, lost in a world beyond my understanding. 'Tis strange to me how these lords and ladies say one thing and mean another; how they parade and preen, flatter and fawn, for I am plain in my thinking and cannot dissemble.

These thoughts ran through her head as the muffled sounds of music and enjoyment came from the great hall. Occasionally a door would open and a messenger would come helter-skelter down the gallery, making the rich tapestries sway. Or a group of gentlewomen would appear, to gossip and whisper then return to the fray. All this while Mary stayed unnoticed.

What will Raleigh do with me, now that I am no longer of use to him? she wondered. With one grand sweep of the cloak he has secured his deepest desire to be returned to the court, and I am glad for him. But he little knows that his advancement produces danger for the Queen, for his success brings Hugh Trevor and his men a step closer to their target . . .

This knowledge disturbed Mary greatly. Until now she had not realised how real the danger was; perhaps Raleigh would never regain his court position, or perhaps the plotters would be discovered by some unseen means. But events had moved on and at any moment Trevor might make his next move. She guessed that his masters in Rome would quickly command him to offer Raleigh huge rewards for turning traitor. Would Raleigh's head be turned by an Earldom, or would he stay loyal to his fickle Protestant Queen, from whose favour he had fallen once before?

She felt she must act, but then once again the raised hand and the fatal dagger appeared in Mary's mind's eye and she heard the whispered warning of her dear father. 'Do not mention Trevor's name in this, or else he will turn on you and have you killed!'

Raleigh will not turn traitor, she told herself firmly, trying in vain to reassure herself. He worships his Queen as if she were the sun who lights his very day.

But perhaps he would weaken under the temptation of wealth and power. And what if the Queen were indeed fickle with her favour, as it was rumoured? Raleigh would have to keep ahead of his rivals by any means: by his wit and good looks or, if that were not enough, by blackening the names of others, by false accusations, or worse.

It was no good; the more she tried to foresee the future, the more out of her depth Mary grew.

If only Hal were here, she thought. We should work out a plan together and act. *He* would keep me safe.

At last, Mary broke out of her reverie and took the only decision she could. I will return quietly to Gresham's house, she thought determinedly, and have Margaret give me back my ordinary clothes. Perhaps she will be kind and tell me of a cloth merchant or a master tailor in the city who lacks a seamstress. Such employment will suit me until I see more clearly what course of action I should take.

So thinking, she slipped out of the gallery by a side door, leaving behind the strains of lively music and the laughter of the great lords and ladies of the land.

Outside she was met by a cold dusk and a damp mist which rose from the river. Across the courtyard, the white canopy of the Queen's barge looked ghostly, while behind her the tall towers and battlements of the house rose sheer and forbidding.

She must hurry on in the dark, along the trampled quayside, with the great river lapping at the wooden jetty and the warning cries of boatmen in cargo-laden boats made invisible by the white fog.

A horse and cart trundled by in the other direction; a cloaked messenger ran out of a side street towards the Queen's house. Mary avoided him by stepping under a rough lean-to shed and letting him pass. Then a second man appeared from the alleyway, looking this way and that along the quayside. He swore quietly, then whistled, while instinctively Mary edged further back, behind a tall stack of baskets used by fishermen for storing their catch.

The whistle brought yet another man from a street further down the quay. The two met and talked, their faces indistinct under brimmed hats pulled low.

'Nothing!' the second man reported.

'Aye, nothing.' The first man strode a few yards up the quayside and then back again. 'She is as slippery as an eel!'

'Or else we were given false direction.' The second searcher was thicker set and seemed more impatient than the first. ' 'Tis a fool's errand to search in this fog. Come, let's leave this until a fitter time.'

'Trevor had her watched; he was certain she would come this way,' the first man muttered, coming nearer to Mary's hiding place.

She shrank back, the name of Hugh Trevor making her clasp her hands over her mouth lest she cry out. They were searching for her!

'Leave it, I say.'

'And let her escape a drowning until the day is clear and every man can see what we do?' the original searcher said scornfully.

'There are other ways to kill a cat besides drowning.' By now the second man had taken to leaning against a wall, his cloak gathered close around him. 'I'm for the ale house!'

he decided suddenly, pushing himself clear and striding off.

Taking a swift kick at the pile of baskets where Mary hid, the first man admitted defeat. 'And I'll follow!' he grunted. 'Trevor may search himself and play the murderer, while we deal with matters more important than seeking out such small fry!'

'Father, Trevor will have me killed!' Mary whispered, her hands together in prayer. 'He has guessed everything. My silence no longer protects me!'

Still shaking and scarcely believing what she had heard from Hugh Trevor's men, she had crept back to Gresham's house and sought her bedchamber. Though she knew that this place was no longer safe, she fell on to her knees to pray aloud. 'Dear Lord, protect me, I humbly beg. I admit my sins and am ready to join my dear father and mother in heaven if it is Thy will. But I would live a little longer, for my sovereign's sake, for there is grave danger to her and those close to her! I must warn Raleigh and take the consequences, Thy will be done, Amen!'

Quickly she rose and took off her silk gown, stepping into her plain grey kersey dress and releasing her hair from its golden clasp.

But before she had time to gather the heavy cloak which she had worn during the ride from Saltleigh, the housekeeper, Margaret, interrupted her.

'Why do you talk of danger?' she demanded in her sternest voice, barring the door against Mary's exit.

' 'Tis nothing,' Mary gasped hurriedly.

'You were at prayer and you talked of warnings,' Margaret insisted. 'What has Raleigh done now that endangers the Queen?'

'You should not eavesdrop on one who prays!' Seizing her cloak, and dropping her plan to ask the housekeeper's help, Mary tried to push past.

The older woman thrust her back. 'If it concerns that vain fool, Raleigh, then it draws in my master too,' she pointed out. 'And if Gresham is hoist by the same petard as Raleigh, then his entire household suffers.'

Mary shook her head. 'I cannot tell you. Believe me, I must seek out Raleigh. There is no time to lose!'

'Child, I do not know what game you are playing,' Margaret said. 'I have watched you since you came to this house and for a time I judged you to be a scheming adventuress using your fresh charms to ensnare a rich man such as my master. But then I saw a mere simple girl caught up by chance in a world far beyond your understanding, and for that I felt sorry.'

'I am the latter!' Mary protested vehemently. 'In faith, I never had designs upon any man, for I would not know how.'

'And yet you let them dress you in silk,' the housekeeper reminded her slyly. 'Methinks they would not so reward you without a reason.'

' 'Twas the cloak!' Mary cried. 'And that alone. I stood my ground and made certain that there was no other reason. And now the cloak is trampled in the mud and my heart is broken and I am defenceless!'

Mary's sudden bout of sobbing brought Margaret round. She drew the child to her and stroked her hair as footsteps sounded on the stairway and Gresham himself burst in.

'Mary, the Queen calls for you!' he announced, bursting with excitement. 'Come, the dancing is over and you are to appear before her in her private chambers. You must not delay!'

'The Queen?' Margaret released Mary and smoothed her crumpled dress.

'Do not echo me, madam. Give me the girl, make way!'

'No, sir, let me make her ready.' Resisting her master, Margaret unlaced Mary and made her stand in her shift while she fetched her silk gown.

But Gresham seized Mary's arm and dragged her to the door. 'There is no time for finery. Come, child, wrap yourself in your cloak and hurry to the Queen.'

'She is barefoot,' Margaret protested. 'Her hair is all undone!'

'Aye, and we shall *all* be undone if we make Elizabeth wait,' Gresham muttered, almost sweeping Mary off her feet and bodily carrying her from the house.

Margaret rushed after them, running along the quay

until they reached the royal house. 'Child, guard your tongue when you go before the Queen!'

'Of course she will guard her tongue,' Gresham countered, setting Mary free and straightening his doublet. 'Why would she not?'

The housekeeper ignored him and tried to smooth Mary's curls. 'Play the innocent,' she insisted. 'There are more forces at work here than you or I can understand.'

Nodding, Mary took a deep breath. Then the great carved doors opened and she was brought in before the Queen.

'Why, child, what made them bring you without your clothes?' Elizabeth asked, with Raleigh at her side.

She sat upon a gilded throne topped by the crowned head of a lion and two pure gold orbs. Inside the tight curls of her red hair nestled hundreds of pearls, and large rubies formed a necklace around her slender white throat. Her gown shimmered silver and her bejewelled slippers rested on a Turkish rug of rich and intricate design.

Before Mary had time to rise from her deep curtsey and find a simple answer to the question, the monarch descended from her throne.

'She is a child of nature, Walter. Did you ever *see* such raven hair?'

'No poet could do it justice, Ma'am,' Raleigh answered. 'They would speak of silken tendrils and the sheen of a blackbird's wing, but still they would not capture it.'

'Her feet are bare,' the Queen said musingly as she walked full circle around Mary. 'She shivers.'

'Your heart is soft as the sweetest pillow of goose down,' he ventured. 'Sweetened with lavender and perfumed by the rose!'

'Aye, and you may keep your similes for the page on which you pen your poems,' Elizabeth rebuked him teasingly. 'There are too many flowers in your speeches, Walter. A woman would soon tire of them.'

Raleigh bowed and fell silent.

'You are Mary Devereux,' the Queen said, turning her full gaze back on the visitor, but seeming to have a faraway look in her eyes. 'Walter tells me you do fine needlework.'

Mary nodded without looking up.

'And you are without a patron?'

Again Mary nodded.

There was a pause before the Queen went on. 'My sister Mary and I learned needlework from the great French instructors. We knew cutwork and strapwork, flounces and gobelins, stitches from every country. Each morning we would sit at our frames with our lengths of thread and the pattern books of Peter Quentel and Frederico Vinciola at our sides, and Monseigneur Henri Charles would scold us if our gaze strayed through the window to the forest beyond, where our father rode and the huntsmen's trumpeters blew.'

Glancing up at last, Mary saw Raleigh give a warning sign that the Queen should not be interrupted.

'That was a happy time. Even now when I sit at my stitching I can recall those days and it brings me a little peace.'

How unhappy she is, Mary realised, then trembled in case there was heresy in her thought.

Elizabeth took Mary's hand and seemed to examine her small fingers. 'Do you know split stitch and stem stitch, Mary?'

'Aye, Madam.'

'And eye stitch and satin stitch?'

'Aye, Madam.'

'And should you like to sit by me while you work?'

Mary hesitated then ventured a glance at the Queen's small face with its high forehead; at the fine lines visible under her eyes and around her mouth. 'I should,' she said quietly.

Elizabeth turned to Raleigh. 'She has a bold look, Walter. Tell me again: where did you find her?'

'At my uncle's house, Ma'am. He is Sir Sydney Campernowne at the Saltleigh estate in South Devon.'

'I know the name, and I have seen the wife, whom I much disliked,' the Queen said, dismissing the subject. 'Now Mary, should you like to live within the city walls, where there is smoke and noise and the constant comings and goings of a hundred thousand souls?'

'I do not know, Madam, for that is new to me.'

'A plain answer, Mary. You would like the grand houses of the Strand, I trust, whose gardens run down to the river, and of Islington and Chelsea, surrounded by pastures that would remind you of home.'

'I should, I think.'

'See how your little seamstress replies, Walter. Her eyes are so serious and clear, I swear you can see into her soul.'

Raleigh came forward. 'I have always found her honest, Majesty.'

Elizabeth turned, walked away, then came back. 'Then I shall steal her from you,' she decided. 'Henceforth, Mary Devereux, you shall execute fleurs de lys and the royal coat of arms. You shall embroider golden owls and white roses, great stags and lions, eagles and griffins: the very stuff of dreams!'

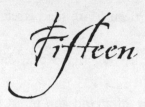

Fifteen

' 'Tis the greatest honour of all,' Mary was told. 'The Queen has bestowed on you the highest favour and in return she will expect absolute loyalty.'

'Aye, you must never speak to strangers of what you see and hear at court, for such talk would be treachery and you should not escape with your head.'

'What is more, you must act with the utmost gentility. You must cast off your old customs and understand that in no way should a woman resemble a man as regards her ways, manners, words, gestures and bearing. You must strive towards a certain soft and delicate tenderness with an air of feminine sweetness in every movement.'

Outwardly Mary accepted such gentlewomanly schooling, as well as the great honour the Queen had afforded her. Inwardly though, she protested against the restrictions the court imposed. Still, she told herself, her unexpected fortune kept her safe from the sinister grasp of Trevor's men.

'That is why stitching is a noble art,' the ladies-in-waiting explained. 'To sit at the frame and draw thread through silk signifies good breeding. Why, 'tis said that King William's Queen Mathilda herself did work on the Bayeux tapestry!'

Mary sat silently at her work, holding back her resentment.

'We women are of a cold and moist humour,' ran the argument. 'We are creatures of feeling, and have not the physical strength of men.'

Aye, but we have full as much courage, Mary thought.

'Bend your neck more gracefully, child,' Lady Mabel Jonson advised. The Queen's long-time companion was dressed in a high ruff and long stomacher, her sleeves embroidered with unicorns and oriental figures. She carried a cream lapdog under her arm. 'Hold not your head too proud, for you are low-born and must show gratitude in your bearing.'

'Neither let your temper appear in your eyes,' the Countess of Essex advised. 'Rather, cover your expression as it were with a mask, so no man may guess your thoughts.'

During all the remaining days of January and into February, and despite the turmoil of her inward feelings, Mary tried to please. She seldom saw the Queen, and almost as rarely Raleigh, who was by now held firmly in the core of Elizabeth's affections. Instead, she kept to the withdrawing rooms furthest from the Queen's public reception rooms, learning yet more tricks with the needle and accepting the dresses and cloaks bestowed upon her so that she should be fit to appear beside the other ladies of the court.

'You see how the Queen has set the cat amongst the pigeons,' Lady Mabel observed to her small coterie of sewing companions one morning in early February when the frost lay crisp on the ground. It was more than a week since Elizabeth had put in an appearance to sit with her needlewomen, and there was an air of boredom in the chamber.

'Raleigh being the cat?' Lady Isabella Dubois inquired with a knowing smile.

'King of Cats!' Lady Mabel laughed. 'He prowls and stalks about the court like a lion in the jungle.'

'Do you see how Leicester takes it?' another added in a high, haughty voice. 'He can scarcely veil his jealously.'

'He grows thin. They say he cannot eat for envy of Raleigh.'

'And how would *you* feel if a rival almost thirty years your junior took your place at the Queen's side?' Lady Mabel challenged. 'Why, the Master of Horse has had his nose put out of joint by a callow flatterer with fine legs and a black beard!'

As the gossip swelled and filled the room, Mary took care not to join in with a defence of Raleigh.

'You know that the Earl of Leicester has devoted his life

to Elizabeth,' Lady Isabella reminded them.

'Aye, a man who has his first wife killed so that he might perchance marry a Queen is devoted indeed,' came a sour rejoinder.

'Tut, 'twas an accident!'

'Amy Robsart fell downstairs!'

'Aye, with a lusty thrust from behind to aid her!'

The gossip ran like wildfire around the room.

Lady Mabel put a stop to it with yet another juicy tidbit. 'I hear that Leicester once confided in the Spanish ambassador that he would bring England back to Catholicism if the ambassador would help him to win Elizabeth's hand!'

'The man would stop at nothing!' Lady Isabella sighed. ' 'Tis well that Leicester has now cast off his allegiance with Rome and consorts instead with Walsingham.'

'Better still if he knew not to meddle with politics abroad, and to serve his Queen more sincerely,' was the final opinion.

All this while Mary had tried to place the Earl of Leicester in her own mind. She asked for more information, but it wasn't until that afternoon that she was given a clear picture of a thin, elderly man with a greyish-red pointed beard and a pinched look about his features.

'The Queen desires the attendance of Lady Isabella Dubois and the girl called Mary Devereux on her visit to

West Cheap,' a stately male visitor to the ladies' sewing room announced.

'There is the answer to your question,' Lady Mabel whispered to Mary. 'Poor Leicester; he stuffs his thighs with bombast, but there's no disguising his thin shanks!'

However, Mary was caught up in the hurry to join the Queen on her outing, and soon she and the young, stylish Lady Isabella were seated on horseback near to the front of the Queen's procession through the London streets. Just ahead of her rode Raleigh with three other gentlemen, and ahead of them, Elizabeth herself.

'How now, Mary!' Entering a maze of narrow lanes, Raleigh turned to address her. 'I would hardly know you in your finery.'

She replied with a guarded smile.

'Ha, she is grown haughty!' he laughed. 'You know that we ride to market to buy emeralds for the Queen? I suggested that you came to sample city ways.'

Mary nodded. 'I thank you, sir.'

'Why thank me for dragging you through the foul-smelling streets, Mary? You see they run with filth from the overflowing cesspits. 'Tis England's shame that her citizens live up to their knees in mire from their own slop buckets!'

'Hush!' Lady Isabella warned, aware that the Queen had turned her head and noticed them.

'You know what is the colour of emeralds, child?' she asked Mary in her loud, imperious voice.

'They are green, Madam.'

'Aye, a clear, sparkling green like nothing else in nature. Green signifies love and joy, does it not, Walter?'

'Aye, as a subject's love for his sovereign and joy in his service to her!' came the quick reply.

Seemingly content, the Queen passed on along West Cheap with her retinue, towards an old, square building supported on wooden pillars. It was thronged with people who wove between the pillars and up stairways to a higher level of walkways where merchants displayed their wares. Above this storey rose three more, all showing gilded signs, with open shutters and candles glimmering within.

'We seek Francois Couthe!' a page leading the royal procession announced as they reached Goldsmith's Row. 'Her Majesty demands to see the pendant of gold embellished with emeralds, fashioned in the shape of a mighty galleon, which she bade him make this New Year past!'

There was a flutter and a flurry as messengers hurried to bring the jeweller down on to the street.

'Now, Mary, look around,' Raleigh instructed. 'Here you see your haberdashers and milliners selling bracelets and brooches, fans and garters. And here your seller of pincases and combs, your shoemaker with his pumps and boots.'

Mary took in the shop windows piled high with goods, the comings and goings, the twists and turns of the city streets. She saw Leicester waiting at the front with the Queen and the jostle of a crowd, mainly women, who gathered to stare.

Then the jeweller was brought before the Queen: a tall man in a long cloak with a heavy brown beard and hair which curled down to his shoulders. About his neck he wore a magnifying glass suspended from a yellow ribbon and in his hand he carried a small silver box with a hinged lid.

'This is Francois Couthe!' the page announced, as the man bowed low.

Without a word, the Queen held out her hand for the box. She remained silent as she opened it and examined the brooch within and, still without a word, flung it on to the ground.

There was a gasp. No one moved to retrieve the precious object. Couthe stood aghast, his face pale, his eyes staring.

'I have seen finer emeralds on the hem of my Master of Horses' cloak!' the Queen spat out, jerking on her horse's reins. 'He who says they are fit for a Queen shall be thrown in the Tower till he comes to his senses!'

Several pages moved in to lay hold of the trembling jeweller until Leicester held up a restraining hand. 'Make the brooch anew,' he advised Couthe, gesturing that he should pick it up and make himself scarce. 'I am to blame, Majesty,' he said soothingly as the royal procession reformed and set off back along West Cheap. 'Next time I will visit the shop myself to ensure that the work is perfect.'

Elizabeth rode with her head high, her back straight as a pike staff. 'Next time I will send Walter,' she told him curtly. 'He knows my taste better than you, Robert, for you are old and out of the fashion!'

It was a jaunty Raleigh that returned to the palace that day. Relaxed and confident, he flattered the Queen and chatted with her ladies-in-waiting, calling Lady Isabella his French rose, then slowing his horse to ride at Mary's side.

I have news from my uncle in Saltleigh,' he told her casually. 'A letter came a week since.'

'Is the news good or bad?' she asked eagerly.

'There's nothing either good nor bad in itself; it's merely the manner in which you look at it,' he hedged. 'For instance, Lady Anne Campernowne fell ill with the fever upon her return to Devon and promptly died, leaving a widower to grieve. Now, to me there is no cause for sorrow, for the world is well rid of the shrew.'

With a sharp intake of breath Mary learned that her old mistress was dead. But what Raleigh said was true; though she was shocked, she would not weep for Lady Anne.

'What of Jayne?' she asked.

'She lives still,' Raleigh told her. 'Her life hangs upon a thread finer than those with which you sew, Mary, but her father prays for her and she may well be spared. The same may not be said for the servants who also fell ill to the fever, and at this moment fight for their lives.'

There was silence then, except for the heavy fall of the horses' hooves.

'Saltleigh is another world, is it not?' Raleigh asked Mary. 'They are yesterday's people, yesterday's events. We move now with the up-and-coming, at the centre of a world where reputations are made and ruined, fortunes won and lost!'

Mary frowned. 'Is my Uncle David among those who fell ill?' she asked. 'And what of Bess and Marion?'

He glanced at her in annoyance, then shrugged. 'Take my advice and don't look back, Mary. Look forward, for the future is there for you to grasp!'

'The Queen is out of temper!' Word ran around the palace. 'She chides and finds fault with her Gentlewoman of the Privy Chamber for mislaying her day book, she throws ale into her chef's face and quotes Greek and Latin at the ignorant grooms, then flies into a fury when they fail to obey her commands.'

'The Queen is the Queen and may do as she wishes,' everyone acknowledged. The foolish stayed and tried to soothe her spirits while the wise made themselves scarce.

'The Queen is often out of temper,' Raleigh acknowledged to Mary in private. It was two days after the visit to the goldsmiths and, wearied by enforced idleness, he had sought Mary out.

'She has shown me great kindness,' Mary pointed out as they walked indoors between chambers decked with giant tapestries and portraits. Looking down at her silver skirt and embroidered shoes, she thought of how things might have been. 'I was saved from making my way in a friendless world.' And from falling into the hands of Trevor and his men, she thought.

'The Queen is kind and cruel by turns,' Raleigh said, staring through a tall window at a frozen garden made up of a maze of low hedges and clipped holly trees. 'The affairs of state weigh heavy on any man, and Elizabeth is but a frail woman.'

'Do not let her hear you say so!' Mary laughed, making her companion smile.' Then I warrant you would not find her frail!'

'I see that in private your spirits are not quite subdued,' he remarked, 'though you begin to wear the courtly mask in public.'

Mary was surprised to hear this. 'I have not changed,' she protested. 'My thoughts are still my own!'

'Bravely spoken!'

'You do not believe me?' Bridling, Mary took her courage into her hands. 'Shall I tell you of my most secret thoughts?'

'If you wish. But remember, there are forces at work here over which you have no control. A whisper in the wrong ear can put you in great danger. Will you still entrust me with your secrets, Mary?'

'Do not mock, sir.'

'I do not. Come outside; we will talk there.'

So saying, Raleigh led Mary into the frozen maze and walked her briskly up and down. 'Now, what is it you would tell me?'

'It is about Rome, sir,' Mary began, realising even as she spoke that her words scarcely carried the ring of conviction. She paused, then stammeringly went on. 'There is a conspiracy among the Catholics.'

Raleigh laughed out loud. 'This is not news, Mary. Why, the wolf of Rome howls at every door in England!'

'But this comes near the throne,' she insisted. ''Tis because of it that my dear father died!'

'Ah now, I see!' Raleigh stood with his hands on his hips, rocking with amusement. 'The master tailor at Saltleigh is implicated in a plot against the Queen!'

'My father was no traitor, sir!' Mary shot back. 'He died because he was a loyal Protestant!'

'So; the master tailor loses his life to defend the Queen!' Still smiling, Raleigh walked on between the frost-covered hedges. 'And who at Saltleigh conspires against her?'

''Tis Hugh Trevor, sir!' There; it was out in the open. The name had escaped from her lips. The deed was done.

Raleigh stopped again. 'Now Gresham's steward?'

'Aye, him. He and two others raised their hands against my honest father. They stabbed him to the heart when he overheard their plot to bring back a Catholic King, then they set fire to my uncle's workshop!'

'Child, child!' Raleigh sighed. 'I see sorrow has pushed you out of your wits.'

'I am not mad!' Mary cried. 'I never was more certain in my life!'

'And I am certain, Mary, that you have no understanding of what you say.' Suddenly Raleigh grew more serious. He took her hand and led her deep into the maze. 'You must not repeat this, nor give it air to breathe and catch light. In other words, Mary, you must put it out of your mind!'

'I cannot, sir, for 'tis true!'

'Mary, forget it. Close the door on it, I say.' Gripping her hand, he walked on. ' 'Tis impossible that it is the truth, for you would not be alive to tell me!'

Mary had to half run to keep up with him. 'Sir, they have tried to drown me at Greenwich, but I stayed well hidden. Before that, I was employed to work on your cloak and they dared not touch me then!'

'More madness!' Raleigh muttered, yet he was evidently distressed by Mary's story. 'What has my cloak to do with a gang of murderers? Tell me, for the life of me I cannot make it out!'

Just then, however, they were interrupted by a shout from the street, and they glimpsed a figure whose head and fashionable feathered hat were just visible above the wall.

'Raleigh, 'tis me; your friend, Gresham!' a voice cried. 'Why, man, you are so high in Fortune's favour that they will not let me talk with you!'

'Gresham!' Raleigh answered crossly. 'Come to the gate and we will speak through it.'

A minute later they had accomplished this unplanned meeting and Mary was forced into angry silence.

'Why so hasty?' Raleigh asked Gresham, speaking through the bars of the gate. 'And why the unkempt beard and lacklustre eye? Do you spend your nights drinking and wenching instead of sleeping?'

'Indeed, I would if I could,' Gresham complained. 'I am come to give you bad news, Walter. My extravagance has brought me to ruin and my debtors hammer continuously at my door. My father must not discover this, so I am come to beg you, as my friend, Walter, to pay my creditors and release me from my debts!'

Raleigh stepped back out of reach of the young student's clutching hand. 'As your friend, Gresham, my answer is no.'

'But you cannot refuse!' the other stammered. 'Walter, I opened my house to you. What I had was yours!'

'Aye, when we both lived on borrowed money,' Raleigh said sarcastically. 'I have risen since then, and you have not.'

Staring in disbelief, Gresham watched Raleigh retreat. 'You jest, do you not?' he implored, his lips trembling into a forced smile, his hand shaking.

Raleigh stared back at him. 'Go to your father, Gresham, and beg on bended knee. Sell the house in Greenwich and live on the capital. Do as you please, for I do not care for you – now or ever!'

Leaving Gresham speechless and beckoning for Mary to follow him, Raleigh strode away. But then he seemed to have second thoughts and he turned again.

'Oh, and by the way, Gresham; now that you are penniless, you will have no need for servants.'

'Raleigh, for God's sake, man! If this is a jest, stop now!'

At the word 'servants' Mary's heart missed a beat. She knew in an instant what Raleigh was about, and it struck her to the quick.

' 'Tis no jest,' Raleigh insisted. 'As I say, you must let your servants go, and I ask you one favour.'

'What is it?' Gresham gasped, his face drained, his figure slumped against the gate.

'I beg you tell Master Hugh Trevor that your star is on the wane and a new position awaits him in the retinue of Walter Raleigh. Impress upon him that I find myself at the very heart of court life, and I am certain he will not hesitate to join me forthwith in loyal service to the Queen!'

Sixteen

'When sorrows come, they come not separately, but in great hordes,' Lady Isabella Dubois told Mary.

Fresh news of the Spanish wars had circulated around court: the enemy's armada ruled the sheltered western Mediterranean sea, guarding the narrow entrance and forcing the English and French out into the wide ocean beyond. Winter storms had persuaded even the bravest adventurers to seek calmer waters, but the Spanish had kept them from their coastal waters and many ships were lost on the rocks.

'They say the "Anne Archer" is among them,' went the gossip. 'Gilbert's ship is sunk off the coast of Spain and all hands lost.'

Mary's cry of despair had drawn the young lady-in-waiting's sympathy and she had consoled Mary while she sobbed.

'My beloved cousin sailed with Gilbert for the Americas,' Mary had confided. 'If he is dead, I have none left in this world to love!' Then she had told Isabella of her father's death by fire and her mother's drowning, and how she had been hounded out of Saltleigh, and hinted that, had it not been for Walter Raleigh, she would not now be alive.

'Child!' Isabella sighed now. 'Your heart is heavy, and no wonder. But we all bear sorrows in this life and must pray to God to protect us and take us into His arms when the light dies and we must take our final rest.'

'God did not protect my cousin Hal!' Mary sobbed, only to be taken by the hands and shaken.

'Hush! We are not to question His ways.' Lady Isabella was more devout than she seemed, in her low-cut gown and tight bodice and with her dainty French manners. She was a tall, slender woman with fair hair and grey eyes, not above eighteen years old but already twice married. 'Come, we will walk in the garden and pray together, you will tell me of your past and your hopes for the future.'

Fetching their cloaks, Isabella and Mary sought out the knot garden for their winter stroll. Under a clear blue sky, and with a carpet of pure white snowdrops spread beneath their feet, they talked of home.

'See these nodding blossoms,' Lady Isabella pointed out. 'How brave they are to show themselves in this harsh English climate! In the south of France a warm wind from Africa protects us all the year round. Grapes grow in great profusion up the walls of the chateaux, our houses are open to the sun.'

'Did you live beside the sea?' Mary asked curiously.

Isabella nodded. 'Until I was fourteen and came to England to be married. Oh, how I loved the sound of the waves against the rocks!'

Mary stopped amidst the low hedges and snowdrops. 'Are you sick for the sight of your home?' she asked, thinking longingly of Saltleigh.

'Every day. But I have a son and a daughter here, and a new husband. How can I return to France?'

Mary was amazed. 'I did not know you had borne children. Where are they now?'

'They live in Northumberland with their father, my husband, Sir Robin Guiseley. The Queen permits me to journey there to visit them whenever she can spare me,' Lady Isabella said, as cheerfully as she was able. But the sadness of separation showed through.

'And does the honour of serving the Queen outweigh the sorrow you feel?' Mary asked, sensing that she would receive an honest reply.

Isabella thought for a while. 'There is no greater honour in this world than to serve a sovereign,' she insisted.

'And yet?'

'And yet my heart is broken in two, nay, in three pieces, when I think of my babies and of my beloved France.'

The young woman's sighs mingled with Mary's as they walked on hand in hand.

'I find solace in Nature,' Isabella confessed, pulling her cloak around her as they approached a more public section of the garden where others walked.

Mary agreed. 'Nature has been a mother to me,' she explained simply. 'She comforts me with her birdsong and shelters me under her green leaves.'

Isabella smiled softly. 'You must work these snowdrops into your lace collars and cuffs,' she suggested, stooping to pick two or three flowers. As she stood up, she came face to face with the Earl of Leicester and a companion, so she curtsied low and Mary did the same.

The men bowed then walked on, deep in conversation.

'Poor Leicester, he must rue the day that he spoke for Raleigh!' Lady Isabella laughed, returning to court tittle-tattle. 'You see, he walks with Walsingham; the two console each other over the loss of Her Majesty's favour.'

Glancing over her shoulder, Mary made out the back view of a tall and graceful courtier beside the stooped, thin figure of Leicester. 'Why did the Earl wish to promote Raleigh if he longed to keep the Queen to himself?' she asked.

Isabella laughed louder. 'Child, the Queen has many favourites, and Leicester knows that he is worn out, like a pair of old slippers. So he must supply other, more handsome and brave young men to make her content. He is wise enough in the affairs of state to know this, yet as a man he is subject to the normal jealousies of a defeated rival. And so he poisons himself to feed the Queen!'

Mary grimaced. 'They are all afraid, are they not?'

Isabella nodded.

'Of the Queen?'

'Aye, for she imprisons many and keeps spies about her. She trusts no one.' Quietly and smoothly Lady Isabella drew Mary to one side to let more courtiers pass. Above them, a blackbird sat in a pollarded beech tree, its golden beak open and its silvery voice trilling into the clear air.

'Look where Raleigh walks!' Isabella pointed out. 'He is in the sun, but there are shadows on every side. Such is his life here in court.'

Mary sought out her old friend from amongst the stylish crowd. Though his back was turned, she knew him by his height and the angle of his hat. After a while she also made out his shorter, stockier companion as Hugh Trevor.

'What ails you, child?' Lady Isabella asked as Mary stopped and gasped.

'Nothing. I have a dizziness in my head, that is all.' Mary swayed and turned pale.

'Then sit here on this seat a while. I will bring the physician.'

Despite Mary's protestations, the young woman hurried away, while Raleigh and Trevor reached the end of their path, turned and walked towards her.

'Mary!' Raleigh called, recognising her and hailing her across the garden.

She took a deep breath, then managed to stand up, hoping to slip away.

'Not so fast!' Raleigh protested with a glittering eye. He and the steward caught her up. 'Anyone would think you wanted to avoid me, Mary, except that I would not believe you capable of such ingratitude.'

'Sir!' Mary murmured with a shallow curtsey, eyes to the ground.

'Ah, I think I see!' Raleigh seemed to hit upon the solution to the mystery of Mary's reluctance. He played a game with them both, relishing the fear in Mary's eyes and the flicker of black anger which played around Trevor's mouth and then vanished. ' 'Tis you she objects to, steward, for she told me she holds a grudge against you and cannot abide your presence!'

Mary gasped and stepped back against the stone seat, while Trevor's expression scarcely broke from its smooth, meaningless smile.

'Mary says that you suspected her cousin of stealing pearls and wanted him hanged,' Raleigh went on merrily. 'But I say we must put all that behind us and learn to rub along. How about it, Trevor? Will you agree to let the boy escape the gallows? Say aye, for my little seamstress's sake!'

'Hal is dead, sir!' Mary broke out. 'He is drowned with your half-brother, Sir Humphrey Gilbert!'

The news took Raleigh aback, but only for a second. Then he went on in his jesting manner, though his eye fixed Mary with deadly seriousness. 'In any account, Mary, you must learn to love Master Trevor, for he is in my service, and I will not have enmity between you.'

'Don't trouble yourself, sir,' Trevor cut in defensively. 'I am not offended, nor am I by any means the monster that Mary paints me. Young girls have rich imaginations; they believe themselves to be in love, or out of love in an instant. They dream of plots and hangings, they see traitors around every corner. 'Tis their habit to misconceive thus!'

Pale and still dizzy, Mary held her breath. What game was Raleigh playing?

'See, Mary? Trevor holds no grudge in return.'

Seemingly satisfied, Raleigh took up some business with the steward within Mary's hearing. 'It is understood, is it not, that Leicester is to be kept in ignorance of my next meeting with the Queen?'

Hugh Trevor nodded, standing with his arms folded, the picture of silent discretion.

' 'Tis tomorrow morning, at Her Majesty's house in Greenwich; a time and a place which must be kept from the rest of the court,' Raleigh insisted.

'The Earl of Leicester shall not hear of it,' Trevor promised.

'Nor Walsingham, nor Oxford. Her Majesty will give it out that she is to buy Turkey rugs for her floors; a trivial matter. I am to be sent ahead of her to Greenwich. We are to enjoy a private meeting together.' Obviously pleased with his privileged position at court, it seemed Raleigh could not help boasting, even to his servant. 'What case shall we build for my absence, Trevor? Come, give me an alibi!'

'We may say that a slight fever keeps you abed,' the steward suggested. 'But we will smuggle you out before dawn and take you downriver under cover of darkness.'

' 'Twill not be a fever that keeps me abed tomorrow morn, but something or someone else!' Raleigh gloated slyly, attracting glances from others in the garden.

'Aye indeed,' Trevor replied smoothly. 'The Queen does you great honour, sir, to trust you thus far.'

Raleigh smiled, then drew his steward on along the path. 'Aye; I shall be alone with the ruler of half this great globe, Trevor! I shall stand astride the world! 'Tis an opportunity that men would kill for, is it not?'

Vanity had blinded Raleigh and turned his judgment, Mary decided. She had always known him to be proud, cunning and careless, yet had thought him sharp-witted until he had come to court.

He has turned his back on his friend Gresham and stolen his steward, she told herself. He promotes Trevor, though I warned against him. It is as though he *invites* treachery into his heart and deliberately exposes his Queen to danger!

The thought stunned and frightened her, as she lay alone in her bedchamber, where Lady Isabella and the physician had left her with a poultice around her temples.

'She is not strong,' the physician had warned. 'She must keep to her bed until the morrow, when I will come again.'

So Mary rested against her high pillow, staring out from behind a heavy gold damask curtain draped around the posts of her oak bedstead. The dark panelled room was lit by a bedside candle, beside which lay a piece of fine lawn part worked by Mary into a pocket kerchief.

Perhaps Raleigh is already for Rome! she thought. Hugh Trevor has worked his poison into his master's brain and now Raleigh is a secret Catholic, planning to kill the Queen!

Child, child! Mary imagined that she heard the world-weary, sophisticated voice of the court. It reminded her of Lady Isabella. You are simple to think such things. You do not understand the powers at work here, so stay abed and rest.

Yes, Raleigh has turned traitor! she convinced herself. Why else would he employ the conspirator, Trevor? It is too much coincidence!

You are confused, Mary, the court voice sighed. Grief for Hal has weakened your wits.

There was a look in his eye when he jested in the garden!

What look, child? That was merely Raleigh teasing at your expense.

A knowing look. A warning look. A look that said I would pay with my life if I betrayed him.

Mary recalled Raleigh's narrowed eyes; far from the

amused openness with which he used to regard her at Saltleigh. It made her tremble.

Then she shook herself, took up her work and told herself not to think so blackly of her benefactor. Perhaps Raleigh is merely caught off-guard by the Queen's unexpected show of favour, she thought, running a row of plain stitching to catch up a thin hem along the long side of the white square. Trevor has taken advantage of Raleigh's vanity, flattered him and wormed his way into his employ, and Raleigh is no more a traitor than I am.

Mary waited for the knowing voice inside her head to lecture her again, but this time there was silence.

Very well; I shall go with my story to the Earl of Leicester! she decided. He must decide where the truth lies. Impatiently she pulled at the suddenly knotted thread, jerking it sharply until it broke.

'No; I do not know what I should do!' she said out loud with a helpless sigh.

Her breath caught the candle flame, making it flicker and almost die.

Wait until the morrow, the inner voice said. Sleep if you can.

Seventeen

'You are to come with the Queen to choose Turkey rugs,' Lady Isabella informed Mary early next morning. She took a gown of cloth of silver trimmed with ermine from the oak chest at the foot of the girl's bed. 'Her Majesty would not hear talk of your sickness, child, so you must feign health to fulfil her command.'

Mary felt a tremor of cold fear run through her. 'I cannot,' she pleaded. 'I am sick to my stomach and my head spins. Say I am faint and cannot stand.'

'Mary, you must do as the Queen wishes, else you will feel her wrath,' Isabella warned. 'We will fetch you physic to strengthen your limbs. Wrap in warm furs. Come, there is no time for delay.'

Struggling from her bed, Mary tried fresh arguments. 'There are a hundred such as I in the Queen's service,' she stammered. 'Let another girl take my place.'

'She has asked for you by name.'

'But she will forget that she did so. Surely any other seamstress would suffice.'

Isabella drew a shift over Mary's head then began to lace

her into her bodice. 'You must understand by now how the court works, Mary. Elizabeth commands empires and Spain trembles at her displeasure. Her courtiers revolve around her as if she were the centre of the heavenly spheres; her slightest wish is our command. You must not *think* then of disobeying.'

Mary felt the Queen's order fall over her like chains binding her hands and feet. Though she desperately desired not to play any part in Elizabeth's secret assignation with Raleigh, she learned she had no choice and must consent to be decked out in finery to accompany the Queen to Greenwich.

'Shall you come too?' she asked Lady Isabella as at last she stood before the mirror with her black hair dressed high on her head, her face pale as a ghost, though no paste or powder had been used to lighten her complexion.

'I do not have that pleasure,' Isabella replied stiffly. 'My Lady Mabel Jonson has used subtle persuasion to be allowed to accompany the Queen, though she has no eye for the colour and weave of Turkey carpets, I'll be bound.'

There was little time now for Mary to settle her confusion and decide on a course of action. Her suspicions that Raleigh had already sold his soul to the Church of Rome lay uneasily at the forefront of her mind. In any case, she was certain that Trevor was drawing ever nearer to his goal and that he would use his first opportunity to rid himself of her troublesome presence.

Perhaps this very morning his co-conspirators would find the means to snatch her from the Queen's small retinue and murder her. They would lurk in the shadows, their knives hidden beneath their cloaks, their cruel eyes fixed only on her, while Trevor and his other plotters moved in silently on the vulnerable Queen.

'Mary, I say you must hurry!' Isabella chided. 'Here are salts to restore you. Take them quickly, then follow me to Her Majesty's chamber.'

Doing as she was bid, Mary found herself hustled downstairs and along corridors, her feet hardly touching the ground.

'Would that you were coming too!' she whispered to the woman she regarded as her friend as Lady Mabel approached from the opposite direction.

Isabella fussed and smoothed Mary's dress and cloak. 'All will be well,' she soothed. 'I will be here on your return.'

'Is this Mary Devereux?' the older lady-in-waiting demanded imperiously, feigning not to recognise Mary and pushing her from behind into the Queen's presence.

At the last moment, Mary turned to Isabella. 'Speak with the Earl of Leicester!' she implored. 'Tell him to go to the Queen's house at Greenwich!'

The Frenchwoman frowned deeply. 'What say you?'

'Speak with Leicester!' Mary begged, her mind in a whirl. 'Upon the Queen's life he must go to Greenwich!'

'What nonsense does she speak?' Lady Mabel asked impatiently.

Isabella stared then shook her head. 'Explain yourself to Lady Mabel,' she whispered back. 'If 'tis important, you must make yourself clear.'

Then the door was closed and Mary found herself in the Queen's presence and curtseying low alongside Lady Mabel.

'And not before time,' the Queen said abruptly. She was dressed for an outing in a rich crimson-and-silver closed gown worked in large gold motifs of roses, honeysuckle and birds. She clasped crimson leather gloves in one heavily ringed hand, and in her hair she wore a pendant of rubies set with pearls.

'Majesty,' Lady Mabel answered, submissively bowing her head but offering no excuses. However, the glance she cast in Mary's direction showed that she blamed the girl for the Queen's displeasure.

'Who talks of Leicester?' Elizabeth inquired.

'Mary Devereux, Majesty,' the lady-in-waiting replied quickly, sweeping across the polished wooden floor in a gown of black velvet trimmed with sable. 'She speaks in riddles.'

'Leicester was here even now,' the Queen said with a distracted air. 'We told him We did not desire his presence until the morrow, which We believe put him much out of humour, for he left Us with a drooping moustache and hangdog expression, though feigning indifference.'

'You hear, girl? The Earl of Leicester is nearby. Shall I have him recalled that you may speak with him?' Lady Mabel addressed Mary with heavy sarcasm, inviting the Queen to join in with the amusing notion of a low-born commoner commanding the greatest in the land.

Mary shook her head and looked down.

'Time speeds on,' the Queen said impatiently. 'It will not wait, even for Us.'

She led the way regally from the palace, ignoring the courtiers' bows and curtseys and stepping quickly into the coach waiting in a courtyard. With Mary beside her and Lady Mabel opposite, and with only four retainers riding at each corner of the carriage, they set off through the city streets.

Past churches and rows of grand houses, merchants' shops and market stalls piled high with fresh produce, the coach rattled along. The occupants sat in silence, scarcely looking out, each lost in their own thoughts.

Then at last Elizabeth addressed her companion. 'My Lady, you will perceive that We do not intend to choose rugs, for we do not go by the Royal Exchange, where the best woven carpets are to be found.'

'Indeed, Majesty,' Lady Mabel replied, with no sign of surprise or curiosity.

'You are the soul of discretion, are you not?'

'I serve you with my life, Madam.'

'Well then, know that We are bound for Greenwich,' the Queen confided. 'And Mary Devereux, you are here with Us according to the wishes of a certain gentleman, else We should not have trusted you in this business.'

Shrinking under the Queen's gaze, Mary nevertheless knew that her sovereign was talking of Raleigh.

'He is uncommon fond of you,' Elizabeth murmured reflectively.

Aye, or else he means to have me killed along with you! Mary thought with a sharp stab of fear. She took a deep breath to slow her racing heart.

'You will wait in the great hall while We retire to Our withdrawing chamber,' the Queen instructed them with an air of one who can command thunder to crash and lightning to strike. 'When We call for you, We will require your assistance with Our gown, and you will minister to Us according to the role played by My Lady of the Bedchamber.'

Once more Lady Mabel nodded without comment. She sat erect, her eyes avoiding the Queen's gaze, her expression unreadable.

But Mary felt a panic rise within her. The Queen must not be alone with Raleigh! Her brown eyes flashed towards Elizabeth, who returned her gaze with indifference.

Each turn of the coach wheels carried them closer to danger; of this Mary was convinced. Each narrow alley concealed conspirators, and every shadow contained a threat.

The Queen still stared at Mary. 'Do you know what love is, child?' she murmured, softening suddenly.

'I do, Majesty.' Mary answered from her heart. 'I have loved and been loved.'

'By whom?'

'By my dear father and mother.'

'Without conditions and complexities,' the Queen acknowledged. 'Such love is more valuable by far than the purest diamond, and for Us infinitely more rare. Be sure to treasure it.'

With tears in her eyes, Mary nodded.

'It comforts Us strangely to be with you,' Elizabeth told her, taking her by the hand. 'But We see that life at court does not suit you, for you are grown thin and pale, your skin is white as alabaster.'

'Your Majesty, I serve you with all my heart,' Mary insisted, feeling the coach draw to a halt and hearing the coachmen open the door for the Queen to alight.

'The service of a pure heart is dear to me, Mary. I shall not forget you.'

These words, spoken in a tone of fond farewell, pierced Mary deeply, so that she drew Lady Mabel aside and whispered urgently in her ear. 'You must send for the Earl of Leicester!' she pleaded. 'He will protect Her Majesty from what is about to befall her!'

'Still prattling on!' the haughty lady-in-waiting replied, shaking Mary off and hurrying after her sovereign.

Anxiously, Mary ran to follow. By now she suspected even the coachmen and the footmen waiting at the door of the house.

Once inside, more servants approached to take their cloaks, then Raleigh himself appeared.

Seeing him, Elizabeth drew herself up and acknowledged him with only the faintest nod of her head.

Raleigh paused for a moment to catch her eye, then dropped devoutly to one knee. Dressed in a short black gown, adorned with elegant, square-cut black gems, and in cream satin doublet and hose intricately slashed and pinked to show a gold lining, he was the picture of courtly refinement.

'Walter, do not pretend you are speechless!' Elizabeth teased. 'Why, man; you of all my courtiers can find words for every occasion.'

'You do me great honour, Madam!' Raleigh said softly, standing according to her silent gesture. For once he held back his fine compliments and let sincerity shine in his eyes.

Mary watched Elizabeth take his hand and accept a gift from him.

'What is this?' the Queen asked, opening a small gold box. 'You give me diamonds, Walter! Is this not presuming too much?'

Raleigh smiled and confidently took a glittering stone from the box. Approaching a small leaded pane in the nearest window, he began to scratch words into the glass while the Queen watched.

' "Fain would I climb, Yet fear to fall." ' she read aloud when he had finished. She smiled knowingly, then took the diamond from him and wrote in turn.

' "If thy heart fails thee, Climb not at all!" ' Raleigh read.

The Queen turned to him. 'Does thy heart fail thee, Walter?'

He gazed boldly at her.

What was he – traitor or lover? Mary's heart was in her mouth.

'No, Madam,' he said.

'Then come,' she invited, leading him out of the hall into her private chambers.

Eighteen

'I would have words with you, mistress!' Lady Mabel told Mary as soon as the Queen and Raleigh had gone from sight.

'And I with you!' Mary cried, allowing herself to be taken outside where they might speak in private. Whatever scolding she was about to receive from the lady-in-waiting, at least Mary would find the chance to push her plea for Leicester and his men to come. Pray God it is not too late! she thought.

'Are you mad, girl?' Lady Mabel began in an icy voice. 'Why do you talk of Leicester when the Queen wishes for secrecy?'

'She is in danger!' Mary cried. She had no thought now for her own safety. 'There is a plot against her, conceived by Hugh Trevor, who is lately made steward to Raleigh. I fear he is here with his master, lying in wait to kill the Queen!'

Lady Mabel's eyes narrowed. 'To kill the Queen?' she echoed.

'Aye! Here, at Greenwich. 'Tis not safe for her to be alone with Raleigh!' How slow the woman was. Why did she not react and rush to send for Leicester?

Instead, Lady Mabel led Mary through the courtyard to the quayside. 'Tell me, Mary: have you spoken to anyone else about Trevor?'

'I have been too afraid,' Mary confessed. 'I wished to warn Raleigh, but he brushed me aside. As for others; who would believe me if I, a mere girl, spoke of the Pope and the Catholic Church?'

'Who indeed?' By now, Lady Mabel had steered Mary towards the water's edge, her expression changing to one of intense hatred. 'By Our Lady, you have come close to revealing all!'

Mary recoiled then looked quickly around. At her feet the mighty grey river, to either side baskets stacked high on the icy cobbles. She had time to take this in before she felt a sudden sharp push against her shoulder and she slipped over the edge of the quay.

Mary cried and reached out for a handhold before she plunged into the water. She clutched an iron ring used to tie up boats, banging hard against the rough stone wall, but saving herself just in time.

'She is a cat with nine lives!' a voice cried from above, and straining to look up, she saw Lady Mabel with two men dressed in black, the high collars of their cloaks hiding their faces.

Then other feet came running along the quay, and from the boats moored along the wooden jetty still more figures sprang out from under heavy canvas covers, leaping out and running to the steps leading up on to the quay.

Holding her breath, Mary reached out to grab the next mooring ring and then the next, gradually easing herself towards the jetty and safety.

'Forget the girl!' the Queen's lady-in-waiting called, pointing towards the men who had leaped from the boats. 'Here are stronger enemies!'

Then the men on the quayside confronted the men from the boats, fighting with daggers and swords, wrestling to gain advantage and fling their opponent into the river.

Crouching on the jetty, Mary listened to the clash of metal and the brutal shouts. Her head spun and her heart thudded against her ribs, so that she did not see the treacherous lady-in-waiting come down the greasy steps on to the jetty until it was too late.

'Did no one teach you to keep your own counsel?' Lady Mabel said, her voice full of controlled menace. 'Why must you prattle and interfere?'

'You have betrayed the Queen!' Mary gasped. 'She held you close to her heart!'

'The Queen has no heart!' Lady Mabel scoffed. 'That organ was ripped out at birth and in its place sits a block of stone! She has Catholics killed like vermin and forbids our allegiance to Rome!'

Traitor!' Mary flung the word at her, even as the woman loomed over her.

'It seems by some means your message to Leicester got through,' Lady Mabel sneered. ' 'Twas the French Protestant woman who took you at your word, no doubt, and the pitiful loyal Earl bethought himself to send his men here in secret!'

Above them, the fight continued to the sound of groans and bodies thudding against walls and baskets.

'They are too late, however!' A cruel smile appeared on Lady Mabel's face. 'Raleigh already meets with the Queen in private and Hugh Trevor has taken up position in his hiding place in her bedchamber!'

At this, Mary threw herself towards the woman. Though smaller and weaker, she was more nimble, and as Lady Mabel reached out to seize her, Mary stepped sideways and made her opponent plunge off-balance. For a second the woman almost regained control, but there was a thin layer of black ice on the smooth wooden boards and she lost her footing. Mary saw silent horror on her face as she slipped and toppled. There was no scream as she plunged into the water; only the billowing of her silk petticoat and a wild reaching out with both arms.

'She cannot swim!' Mary murmured in sickening realisation.

The woman's heavy black gown soon saturated and dragged her down, arms stretched wide now, hair loose, and her pale face disappeared into the grey swirls of the great river.

Mary turned away. She climbed the steps and found that the skirmish on the quayside continued. Three men lay motionless on the ground, while five more fought on, their faces and hands running with blood.

Quickly she slipped past them, hollowed out with shock, her head dazed but still carrying one goal in her mind.

I must reach the Queen! she told herself.

But it must be by stealth, for there would be footmen and servants whom she could not trust. Lady Mabel Jonson had proved false and had paid for it with her life. But there might still be other conspirators dressed in the guise of loyal followers. Yes; she would enter the house by a back door and seek out Elizabeth.

Breathing hard, her body aching from the bruises she had received, Mary crept into the house and along the servants' corridors, up the narrow staircase which she knew led to the minstrels' gallery. From there she paused to look down on the hall where the ladies and gentlemen of the court had danced, leaning over and checking under the gallery to make sure that no conspirators had forced an entry. When a door at the front of the hall opened, she withdrew quickly and hurried on.

Concentrating, Mary recalled which part of the house was used for the Queen's private audiences and began to pick out a route along corridors and down more steps towards it.

I could call out for help and now I would be believed, she told herself. There is the evidence of the traitors' corpses on the quayside. And yet, Raleigh and Trevor were with the Queen at that very instant. Any alarm from her would push them into instant action. No; staying silent bought her at least a little time.

But the weight she carried was almost unbearable. For the first time she knew for certain that she alone held the Queen's safety in her hands. She must be cunning and quick to outwit Trevor, for it was by stealth that he had succeeded, and by stealth he must be overcome. Somehow she must draw the Queen away from Raleigh and Trevor, and deliver the news of the conspiracy in secret.

Reaching the Queen's withdrawing chamber, she stood in the corridor beneath a huge portrait of a past king. The monarch stood in swaggering pose, one hand on his hip, the broad shoulders of his fur-lined cloak making the figure look square and powerful. The eyes of the portrait seemed to observe her as she took a momentous decision, knocked on the Queen's door and entered.

The Queen and Raleigh sat together studying a book. His arm was around her shoulder; she was leaning into him, her head on his shoulder.

'I did not send for you yet, Mary,' the Queen said quietly, without stirring.

Mary's step faltered. 'Madam, I have grave news,' she stammered.

'Grave enough to place a man six feet under the ground in his "grave" by the look of you,' Raleigh said, only half in jest. Reluctantly he surrendered the book to Elizabeth and rose to his feet to meet Mary. 'Might not it wait until we have done?'

'No, sir.' Terrified, Mary stood her ground. 'Someone is drowned in the river, Your Majesty. Master Trevor would that his master come to see.'

At this Raleigh started. 'Drowned, you say? And the steward has need of me?'

Mary watched him carefully. Would he fall for her trap to draw him away by mentioning Trevor's name?

'Come, come,' the Queen broke in, inviting Raleigh to return to her side. 'A hundred poor souls die so each day. Let it go by.'

But then Hugh Trevor himself entered by a door in the opposite wall. 'A thousand apologies, Your Majesty!' he blustered. 'By no means did I bid the girl come. Her poor wits are turned, I see, and she hears words inside her head which were never spoken!'

'What – is no one drowned?' the Queen asked.

'A beggar woman, Madam,' Trevor lied. 'It need not concern you or my master. But let me take the girl away so that she may cause no more harm.'

Elizabeth sighed then silently sought Raleigh's agreement

before nodding. 'But I pray thee, let her be treated kindly, not harshly,' she advised. 'For she is far from home and in poor health.'

'Your Majesty, no!' Mary protested, resisting Trevor's attempt to grasp her by the arm. 'These men mean to harm you!'

At this Trevor pounced and placed his hand across Mary's face. 'I will stop your mouth, mistress!' he snarled, lifting her off her feet and carrying her to the door. She bit him and made him curse, kicking and twisting in her effort to escape.

'The devil is in her!' the steward cried.

Standing to one side, Raleigh made no attempt to intervene. 'As the Queen said, do not deal cruelly with her,' he advised calmly, one hand across his chest, the other resting lightly on the curved handle of his rapier. 'If the child proves mad, fetch her physic and have her kindly treated, for the fever in her brain may abate and her wits be restored.'

'You hear us, steward?' the Queen insisted, flinching at the sight of Mary scratching and fighting to be free.

'Majesty, I obey your will in every small thing,' Trevor grunted, finally hauling Mary through the door and out of sight.

Locked in his grasp, Mary struggled as the cunning traitor dragged her down stone steps into a cellar containing large casks and wooden barrels. The dark room was lit by one candle in a rough iron sconce which threw long shadows across the stone floor. The flame flickered and almost died as Trevor slammed the door.

'To be almost thwarted in our desires thus!' Trevor cried, flinging Mary across the room. 'By a creeping, sly tailor's daughter who collects secrets as a jackdaw steals bright scraps!'

She fell groaning into a corner, covering her head with her hands and curling her knees to her chest.

'Would that you had died with your father!' the steward went on, for a time beside himself with rage. 'You witnessed his murder, did you not? Come, mistress, tell all, for what profits it now if you conceal the truth?'

'Aye, I saw the knife raised against him!' Mary confessed. 'And I heard you plot the Queen's downfall.'

Roughly Trevor raised her from the ground. 'Aye, the Queen's downfall and the Pope's rise! Before we are done, this land will return to the true path and the Protestant upstarts will be cut down like corn in the autumn fields!'

Mary struggled free and darted towards the door, but Trevor caught her once more and pinned her against the wall.

'Learn then before you die the force of what you oppose. We are many,' he boasted, 'and our people are woven into the fabric of this country from the lowest to the highest. We began in Oxford. Secret meetings were held at the estate of George Carew, alliances were forged between scholars and landowners, poets and merchants. The Earl himself espoused our cause.'

Holding her head in her hands, Mary tried to block out Trevor's revelations. 'What of Raleigh?' she asked, curiosity overcoming her despite her efforts. 'He was in Oxford with George Carew, was he not?'

'Hah, the little seamstress keeps her ear to the ground!' Trevor mocked. 'Think what you may of the Queen's new favourite, for I will not tell you!'

Crying out in despair, Mary made one more lunge for the door, but the steward drew a dagger from its sheath at his waist, pursuing her with scornful words. 'This alliance is what you sought to topple, child. 'Tis a cause for laughter, is it not?'

Mary turned to see the raised dagger. For a moment she was resigned. 'Then welcome, death!' she cried. 'For I would not live in a world where evil triumphs!'

But then the door flew open and a man burst in, crying 'Traitor!' He wrestled the weapon from Hugh Trevor's hand.

Mary seized the chance to escape, fleeing up the stone steps and along the corridor, back to the Queen's private chambers. By now there were others running here and there, setting up cries and rushing out on to the quayside. She ignored them all and burst into the grand withdrawing chamber with its high, ornately carved ceiling and long, paned windows.

Here she stopped for breath. Looking round, she saw the room was empty, though a panelled door leading to an inner chamber was slightly ajar. Without thinking, she rushed towards it and entered the second, smaller room.

In the quiet chamber, Mary found the Queen and Raleigh in a deep embrace. They sprang apart when they heard her enter and Elizabeth fixed her with a furious eye.

'You must flee!' Mary cried, her hair undone and wild around her face, her arms grazed and skirts torn.

The Queen broke free from her lover's arms. 'Fetch the guards!' she told Raleigh. 'We will not endure this!'

'No, no, you must leave this place!' Mary pleaded. Behind her she heard footsteps approaching, though she had no idea whether they belonged to friend or foe.

'Are you raving?' Quickly the Queen strode towards Mary. 'Understand this: We do not flee upon any provocation. We are Queen of this realm and none dares disturb Us!'

'Madam,' Raleigh began, drawing his rapier and advancing towards them.

The fury in Elizabeth's voice did not abate. 'Who dares bare his sword in Our presence?' she cried.

But then the door flew wide and Trevor appeared, dagger in hand. There was blood on his face and cruel determination in his eye. 'Our time has come!' he gasped, wielding the knife above Elizabeth's head.

'Sir, I am your appointed Queen!' she pronounced without a tremor of fear. 'I will never be constrained by violence, for I have as good a courage as any man!'

Crying out wildly, Mary turned to Raleigh. He stood poised, his face deadly pale.

'Prepare to die, Madam!' With a sudden lunge, Trevor moved in on Elizabeth, who stood her ground with her head held high until Raleigh swept her aside. Without a trace of mercy, he thrust the deadly point of his rapier deep into Hugh Trevor's side.

Nineteen

Throughout the early spring of the year 1582, the rotting head of Hugh Trevor was displayed on a spike at Traitors' Gate. His co-conspirators, including a cousin of George Carew and a nephew of the Earl of Oxford, were hanged by the neck until they were dead, their heads removed and similarly displayed as a discouragement to other secret Catholics with desires to remove the Protestant Queen from the throne of England. In all, twelve conspirators were tried and hanged. It was broadly believed that Carew and the Earl were fortunate to have escaped this same fate.

From her house at Greenwich on that fateful day, the Queen rapidly removed to her palace in the city, taking Raleigh and Mary Devereux with her.

'You see now what it is to be sovereign ruler of all England,' she told the courtier who had saved her life as they rode in the carriage through the crowded streets. 'In the end, not all the gold and rubies in this world, nor great armies and navies, nor the worship of Our people can save her from the secret assassin's knife!'

'Yet you live,' Raleigh said, his hand still stained with Trevor's blood. 'Praise be to God!'

The Queen smiled. 'In this present instance,' she said quietly. 'And 'tis thanks to you, Walter.'

A long, wearying sickness kept Mary in bed through the rest of that winter.

Lady Isabella Dubois, having been duly rewarded with extra lands in Northumberland for her part in sending the Earl of Leicester's men to Greenwich, tended her kindly. She brought Mary news from the court and left her with small tasks which she could perform in her convalescence.

'Her Majesty wishes for a cutwork kerchief embroidered with red raspberries around its rim. 'Tis a gift for the ambassador from the French court to take home to his wife. The Queen chose you to execute the work, Mary.'

Stitching the familiar patterns, feeling her needle fly through the fine fabric, Mary felt slowly restored to health.

Yet she was troubled by nightmares, and could not rest easy in London.

'They say that Her Majesty has secretly married Walter Raleigh,' Lady Isabella reported one day with a bright but sceptical smile. ' 'Tis true they are deep in love as any man and woman may be, but I surmise that the Queen is not so impolitic as to make this match.'

Mary looked up from her stitching.

'Don't be surprised, child.' Isabella smiled fondly, rising from the bedside ready to leave. 'These are matches to be made between the thrones of Europe, not between a man and a woman. Love has no part to play.'

'I am sorry for it,' Mary sighed. She remembered the Queen's words: 'Love is more valuable by far than the purest diamond, and for Us infinitely more rare.'

'They say too that Raleigh will soon be knighted, and this I judge to be more than likely.'

Mary nodded.

'Leicester opposes it, however. He listens to the rumours that put Raleigh at the very heart of the Catholic conspiracy, though 'tis acknowledged that he emerged at last as Her Majesty's saviour.'

Mary thought for a while, recalling her old suspicions of Raleigh. 'And do you think these rumours to be true?'

Isabella shook her head and gave a pretty laugh. 'Nay, I cannot judge. 'Tis possible that he joined the plot at first, only to change his mind at the last minute and play the hero instead. There was a fine prize to be gained in that. What do you think, child? You were closer than any.'

'I do not know,' Mary frowned. If Raleigh had been altogether innocent, he had played the riskiest of games. Was it innocence and shrewdness combined that had led him to employ Hugh Trevor and carry the Queen to the very brink of death? Innocent because his loyalty was absolute. Shrewd because he had worked out the very best way to play the hero and so embed himself in Elizabeth's heart. Thus he had gambled with his sovereign's life.

In the end she said to her friend, 'These men are sophisticated. I am too simple. My mind is perplexed.'

Isabella stooped and kissed her cheek. 'Mary, you are the sweetest girl, and would that you were well again and receiving the rewards you deserve.'

'I will not be well until I leave London,' Mary confessed, gazing up at her friend. 'And I do not seek reward.'

Isabella nodded. 'I know,' she sighed, then left Mary to rest.

'The Queen has granted you permission to return to my uncle's estate in Devon,' Raleigh announced one afternoon in early April. He had summoned Mary to a private chamber, having expressed concern at her poor health when he met her by chance walking in the Queen's knot garden with Lady Isabella.

'What ails you, Mary?' he had asked.

'I am sick for the flowers of the forests – for the yellow primrose and the purple violet,' she had confessed.

Raleigh had called it a strange answer, then said it was just what he might have expected of Mistress Mary.

'You may depart as soon as you feel strong enough to make the journey. But are you certain you are ready to give up the Queen's favour and this life of luxury?' he asked her now, studying her closely.

'Her Majesty will find another seamstress more grateful than I,' she replied.

'Aye, but none so skilful,' Raleigh contended, regarding Mary with his old fondness. 'Did I do you an injustice to bring you from Saltleigh?' he asked.

'No, sir. You saved my life.' And she told him how the making of his cloak had kept her safe from Trevor.

'Then I angered you by taking the traitor into my service,' he recalled. 'Poor Mary, you must have thought me a fool . . . or worse!'

She said nothing, but stared directly at him.

'Ah, the eloquence of that gaze!' he sighed. 'To be truthful, child, I did suspect Hugh Trevor even then. But there is a devil allied to vanity in me that is wedded to taking risks. I thought to employ the man, get close to him and learn his secrets. How noble then I would become in the Queen's eyes if I revealed a secret plot against her throne!'

Still Mary held his gaze.

'Do you believe me, Mary?'

'I cannot tell,' she said honestly. 'I only know that the risk was great.'

'Almost too great, I confess,' Raleigh said with a sad smile. 'Men here suspect me and cast doubt upon my motives, but know that I love Elizabeth,' he insisted. ' 'Tis an enduring love, but a hopeless one, for if she marries, 'twill be to a prince and not to a mere poet and adventurer!'

'Does the Queen love you?' Mary inquired.

'Aye, for the present, though I may soon fall out of fashion like an old cloak!'

'Is she so fickle, sir?'

More sadly still, Raleigh contemplated the intricate pattern of low green hedges through the window. 'Her soul is constant, Mary, but like all rulers she is tainted by the power she wields. Even now I see in her eye when I displease her and must humble myself to her command. In the months and years to come, I will see that look grow, until the time comes when it remains and I cannot flatter nor tease her out of it. She will send me abroad to conquer new lands and test my loyalty. 'Twill never be enough. I may die in her service, or else be cast out forever.'

'I cannot believe that,' Mary protested, humbled by his frankness.

'Believe it, child; I shall end my days in the Tower. Until then, wish me happiness!'

'With all my heart,' Mary whispered sadly, at last taking her leave.

Mary never saw the Queen again. Her departure for Saltleigh took place at dawn on the first of May, with pink buds bursting forth on the blossom trees and only Lady Isabella to see her on her way.

She did not look back at the palace. If she had, she would have seen two figures: a woman with long red hair, a dark man with a pointed beard, standing at a long upstairs window, their arms around each other's waists, watching her go.

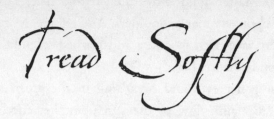

Tread Softly

'Aye, we survived the fever,' David Devereux told Mary upon her arrival at her old home.

Flowers and green moss grew amongst the tree roots around the cottage where she had lived with her mother and father. She strolled here with her uncle, learning about the events of the last four months.

'Marion escaped the sickness, though it claimed a good deal of flesh from Bess's sturdy frame. Only half of her bulk remains, and to tell the truth that suffices!'

'What of Jayne?' Mary inquired.

'You will see for yourself. She has lost a sister and so lacks someone to argue with. She has no mother and misses her scolding. 'Tis a strange, quiet child now.' Slowly David turned back towards the house, into the setting sun. 'Sir Sydney has passed her care into the hands of a nurse and he spends his time in the stables and out on the fields with his new steward, Peter Paley. It occupies him well enough.'

'And you; you have grey hairs!' Mary teased. She did not mention Hal for fear of distressing her uncle.

'I am Master Tailor now,' David told her. 'That is a weight upon any man's shoulders. And tell me, Mary, now that you have been to court and learned splendid ways, shall you be happy here?'

Closing her eyes and breathing in the green smells, feeling the faint glow of the sun upon her cheeks, she answered truly. 'I shall be happier here than anywhere, Uncle.' Slowly making their way, David led Mary into the kitchens for supper. 'Sit and rest,' he advised.

But then Jeremy the cook appeared and drove her into activity. 'Mistress Mary, I fear you are too grand to set out the platters for bread and tankards for beer!'

Seizing the cups, she arranged them on the table.

The cook laughed before he vanished again. 'I will send in the loaves and you may cut them.'

'. . . Fetch and carry, fetch and carry; 'tis all I do from morn till night!' a voice grumbled. 'I must ride to town for fish and to market for flour. Then it's ale from the cellar and water from the well, bread for the table – fetch and carry, fetch and carry . . .'

As Mary listened, her eyes grew wide. Her ears must be deceiving her, or else the ghost of Hal Devereux haunted these corridors!

The bearer of the basket of bread turned the corner. He seemed taller than before and broader across the shoulders but the red hair gave him away.

'Hal!' Mary sprang up with a cry, sudden tears of fear

and joy pricking her eyes. 'Are you not drowned?'

'Oh aye, and my bones have been picked clean on the seabed!' he replied, dumping the bread on the table. 'This is my twin, look you!'

'Hal!' she cried again, embracing him.

'Hold!' he complained, struggling free. 'Who is this lady? . . . Why 'tis my fine cousin! Are you not married to a Spanish duke and become Mistress of the Queen's Wardrobe?'

'Aye, and you must bow down to me and call me My Lady!' she retorted, her heart surging with sudden relief. 'Hal, why are you not smashed to pieces on the rocks?'

'By the grace of God I survived while my captain and most of his crew were lost,' he told her. 'Forty-foot waves do not defeat a Devereux! No; after two days afloat on a piece of driftwood, a Portuguese fisherman hauled me out and rowed me to his village. He professed he liked my red hair and 'twas only by a miracle that I escaped betrothal to his ugly, thin, big-nosed daughter!'

'Hal, Hal!' she remonstrated, hugging him again.

'Be seemly, madam!' he insisted. Then his face broke into a broad grin. 'Welcome back, Mary. I own I am glad to see you.'

'And I to see you, Hal.' She smiled back. 'For I never did think to meet you in this world again, and it pleases me more than I can say!'

'You will stay here, Mary?'

'Aye, if Sir Sydney will employ me. And shall you stay too?'

Hal broke into a loaf and began to chew the crust. 'Not I, coz!'

'No?' Mary sat back on the bench with a disappointed frown.

'Nay, I'm for the Americas!' he vowed, striding to the door and looking south towards the sea. 'When the wind is set fair and the sun rises high in the sky, I'll be gone! For why should I rot here when there is a whole New World to discover!'

In 1585 Walter Raleigh was knighted by Elizabeth I.

In 1603 he was found guilty of treason and thrown into the Tower by James I, where he spent the next 13 years.

He was released in 1616 and sent to find gold in Guyana. The expedition failed.

In 1617 he was executed for treason, dressed in a satin doublet, black embroidered waistcoat, black taffeta breeches, coloured silk stockings, an embroidered hat . . . and a black velvet cloak.

Mary Devereux became a member of the Guild of Master Tailors and was renowned for her skill in the courts of Elizabeth I and James I.

In June 1584 she married Peter Paley, steward to Sydney Campernowne on the Saltleigh estate in South Devon.

There were two sons of the marriage: John and Hal.